ALSO BY JULIE HECHT

Happy Trails to You

Was This Man a Genius?: Talks with Andy Kaufman

Do the Windows Open?

THE
UNPROFESSIONALS

JULIE HECHT

Simon & Schuster Paperbacks

New York   London   Toronto   Sydney

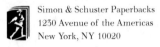 Simon & Schuster Paperbacks
1230 Avenue of the Americas
New York, NY 10020

First Simon & Schuster trade paperback edition August 2008

SIMON & SCHUSTER PAPERBACKS and colophon are registered trademarks
of Simon & Schuster, Inc.

For information about special discounts for bulk purchases,
please contact Simon & Schuster Special Sales at
1-800-456-6798 or business@simonandschuster.com.

Manufactured in the United States of America

10   9   8   7   6   5   4   3   2   1

Library of Congress Cataloging-in-Publication Data

Hecht, Julie.
    The unprofessionals : a novel / Julie Hecht.
        p.   cm.
    1. Eccentrics and eccentricities—Fiction.   2. Women photographers—Fiction.
3. Middle-aged women—Fiction.   4. Women drug addicts—Fiction.
5. Heroin abuse—Fiction.   6. Friendship—Fiction.   7. Young men—Fiction.
8. Telephone—Fiction.   9. Psychological fiction.   I. Title.
    PS3558.E29U57   2008
    813'.54—dc22   2008023657

ISBN-13: 978-1-4165-6427-0
ISBN-10:   1-4165-6427-6

For Nick

CONTENTS

CONTENTS

THE UNPROFESSIONALS

AN EVENING IN WINTER

IT WAS the second month of living without a soul and I was getting used to the feeling. The obliteration of the self had begun two years before—probably it had begun many years before—but now I was at the brink of being seriously over forty-nine and it was coming to fruition.

I saw every mistake I'd made, also the flaws in my character as well as my bone structure, and the combination of the two was deadly, forcing me to drag around the empty shell of a human form like the lost shadows of Peter Pan and Wendy, or Casper the ghost. I dragged this around with my new lack of self and missing soul each day.

Unlike a number of movie stars, I lacked the will to add false cheekbones. There is one early stage of the face falling in that gives the face owner the appearance of having bone structure, but I had acknowledged a while before this newest episode of emptiness and nothingness that the stage of slight structure had already passed, leaving the decline to a face that looked like a soft, still-unformed pancake, nothing more.

Sometimes, passing in front of a mirror, before I'd learned to avoid the dastardly objects, I'd seen the beginning of the pancake effect, and a few times this made me laugh out loud. Not the mad laugh of a woman in an asylum, as in the movie *Spellbound*, but a laugh of disbelief, of incredulousness that this could be happening to me. What had I done to deserve it?

I'd never smoked or drunk alcoholic beverages. I'd taken no drugs. I'd avoided the sun after I found out about it at age thirty—too late. I tried to practice yoga and walked many miles every day. I'd been a vegetarian since birth, and then a vegan as soon as possible after that.

It had to have been the bad thoughts. It must have been my low opinion of my mother's middle-aged face, my not having had the smallest inkling that this same facial decline might lie in store for me—it must have been that for which I was being punished. Also the damage done by the years of forced milk drinking during childhood. This was only the outside—I'd read that damage to the innards begins after infancy. I pictured plaque deposits starting in first grade, when my mother was among those who paid milk money to the teacher so the little cartons of the thick liquid would be delivered to the classroom, where the unsuspecting children would have to drink it.

FOR WEEKS, or years, I'd wished that I had someone to talk to. My closest friend, a twenty-one-year-old boy, was away in rehab for heroin addiction.

My other friends were a group of narcissists or anxiety-depressives. Not that they were in any kind of organized group of people who knew who the others were. The narcissists were too narcissistic to care about anyone else and the anxious ones were too anxious to think about anyone but themselves. I was married to a man who liked to say, "You knew when you married me that I didn't talk."

I'D HAD one good day—or was it just a good few minutes—plus a grand finale that followed: the drive home from the discount drugstore with a bag of Xanax, a bag of chocolate, and, on the brighter side, a bag of Dr. Scholl's gel-and-foam innersoles. At the time I still had the high hopes of walking farther and farther each day.

It was exactly the right time of night to be at the discount drugstore—eight-thirty—too late for children to be running around crying or demanding, in Spanish, candy and plastic toy-like objects, but not close enough to the nine P.M. closing for me to be thrown out before I could gather up all the medium-green Reach toothbrushes with firm bristles.

I had developed one bond with Patrick Buchanan, a man whose every sentence used to infuriate me: I wanted to hear English spoken by cashiers and customers. At least I wanted the cashiers to stop speaking Spanish to each other and help the customers at the counter.

"Good evening, may I help you?" I never heard that. I had heard David Letterman say that when he was a grocery-bagger youth at a supermarket, he used to say "Hello" and "Thank you." He complained during his shows that the clerks and baggers no longer spoke to or even made eye contact with customers. He didn't mention the Spanish. The more Spanish I heard, the more enraged I became. I knew this was another new, bad thing about myself.

I had all the time I needed to look through the Dr. Scholl's innersoles and as I was studying a new light-pink rubbery kind with a miniature waffle pattern I heard a woman's voice say, "Don't get those. They're terrible."

Since I had lived without a mother's advice for many years, I was startled to hear anyone say anything like this to me. I couldn't remember the last thing my mother had told me to get or not get.

"Get Electrasol," she had told me about a dish-washing powder after I was married. "It's far superior," she added with a conviction that was a waste of her intelligence. I'd taken the advice and had bought Electrasol ever after, except for an experiment in switching to Ecover, the ecologically preferred brand. When Ecover didn't remove tea stains from cups, I had to go back to the chlorinated Electrasol. I felt bad every time I reached for the box.

Some weeks earlier, I'd been dismayed to find that the Electrasol corporation had fiddled with the original formula and created a blue "Dual Action" product to replace the single-action white powder. The odor of the blue powder almost knocked me out when I opened the little metal spout on the box. I remember gasping for breath as I staggered out of the cleanser aisle.

When I looked up at the woman who was giving me the innersole advice at the drugstore, I was alarmed. I had seen her on other nights in the half hour before closing time at this drugstore, as well as at the supermarket late at night. Often she and I were the only two customers in either store.

She was around fifty, or even older. She had long black hair, too long for her age, too long even for age forty, long black hair halfway down her back, or maybe hanging a few inches lower than the shoulders of her black leather jacket. Yes, black. Black, the darkest and deadliest of the colors. She was dressed head to toe in this color, yet she thought she should speak to me.

She wore a black T-shirt underneath the black jacket and tight black pants, too tight for her ten pounds of overweight, and to top all this off she wore black shoes—high-heeled shoes—black pumps, they may still be called. I had no way of knowing, since I was no longer reading fashion magazines, even in doctors' waiting rooms. Walking and climbing magazines were my choices.

On her face she wore a load of makeup—black eye makeup for eyebrows and eyeliner, tan powder with liquid face makeup underneath, and then—a final brutal shock to my delicate system—she was wearing bright red lipstick.

I was still weak from the night before, when I'd almost passed out in the cleanser section at the supermarket after stepping into the aisle without even opening the spout on a box of dishwashing powder. The collected chemical fumes from all the detergent boxes were somehow seeping out into the air and I had to flee without even trying to hold my breath long enough to dash up the aisle to get some sponges.

I LOOKED up at the face, the whole personage of the woman customer who had taken it upon herself to advise me about the innersoles, and this is what she said: "You can feel the little square sections on the soles of your feet."

"Oh," I said. "Thanks for telling me."

"Get these," she said, pointing to the plain white foam style.

"They wear out too fast," I said, beginning to feel the shock of being in a conversation with her.

"But they're better," she said. "Get more and replace them."

Apparently she hadn't seen the environmental segment of

the program, *Pinnacle*, I had just watched on TV—it was about getting less. A carpet-company executive had become environmentally responsible after reading a book on the subject—it was "a knife in his heart," or some such dramatic phrase. "I was guilty," he said.

Then he figured out a way to make his carpets last ten years, and during the ten years his company would service and repair the carpets, and when they were beyond repair he'd take them away and recycle them. A gigantic machine was shown grinding up old carpets and spewing out bits of gray and black rubbery stuff into another machine or bin to make more carpets.

The case of Dr. Scholl's in regard to the topic of recycling was as yet unknown to CNN's *Pinnacle* viewers. I pictured the mounds of worn-out and discarded foam shoe pads in a landfill in New Jersey filled with all kinds of garbage, or at the town dump in Nantucket, where a special dome had to be built to keep the ever-expanding waste and accompanying fumes away from the homes of the many new million- and billionaires and their moors-encroaching real estate development. Since almost all of Nantucket was for sale, the land near the dump had some of the best views of the once-beautiful island.

"Oh, okay," I said to the woman in all black. "That's a good idea."

Why hadn't I thought of it myself? I was trying to be ecologically correct. As she finally left—reluctantly, and with a steady and beady-eyed glance at my hand to make sure I wasn't keeping the pink soles—I began to wonder what it was about my appearance that made such a person think she might speak to me and give advice.

I was wearing a big old khaki cotton jacket with a blue-and-green-plaid lining and an older green corduroy skirt with dark green cotton leggings and two-tone green New Balance hiking sneakers. Underneath the coat I had on a worn-out white cotton shirt and an unraveling beige cashmere V-neck cardigan I'd gotten from Scotland before all the good plain things disappeared from stores.

My husband had stopped criticizing or even mentioning that I wore this skirt, shirt, and sweater, or others just like these, every day. I lived in fear that he might mention the subject, but I guessed he'd given up on that after he'd realized that my mental condition couldn't take the burden of any clothes buying.

My hair, I was horrified to notice as I passed the sunglasses-display drugstore mirror, was almost platinum blond, with pieces sticking out from having more and more highlights added in an attempt to lighten and cheer up the area around the pancake face. My skin was pale and white, and the tiny bit of makeup I had on it served only to even out the whiteness instead of enlivening it. The cheek-color makeup had faded away and the no-flake mascara had flaked off during a long hike to the ocean from the snow-covered conservation land, which was rated one of the five most beautiful conservation areas in America.

The summer look was worse, I remembered, when I recalled the initial horror with which I'd viewed my image in a mirror near the product section of a haircutting parlor in Nantucket the summer before. At first I didn't realize the person was myself, or my former self, or the physical form in which the former self had once resided. My beige linen skirt was wrinkled and worn thin from Clorox-washing, my white linen shirt ill-fitting and smashed, and my hair already too light, strawlike, and unkempt. When I saw this image, I left the parlor immediately.

The owner had looked at my hair the week before and said as a reprimand, "Condition is part of color." I reminded him that his partner had done the color.

"But Jim did the highlights," I said. "Tell him."

He looked at me over the top of his yellow-framed reading glasses. No apology was made. That's the world now, or a micro-cosm of it. One person ruins your hair, the partner publicly criticizes it and has no embarrassment upon hearing the truth. "Jim's the culprit," I wanted to add, but feared the matter would get out of hand.

When I first went to Nantucket, in the 1960s, there were no haircutting parlors of this kind—no waxing, massaging, or sea-weed facials. The seaweed was in the sea. At the grocery store there wasn't even any Grey Poupon Dijon mustard, now out-done by hundreds of other mustards. People had to bring their own De Cecco pasta—that, too, now passé. Back then, Ronzoni and Buitoni were the only brands in the two food stores.

At that time everyone else had wrecked hair and rumpled clothing. In the present era I thought I must have been an eye-sore amidst the crowds whose place of spiritual origin was *W* magazine. During this time I wandered without a soul, not knowing or understanding what I had lost.

The feeble attempt at organizing the shell of the self showed in the mirror that day—I could see that even in the geographi-cal place where I'd once fit into the landscape, my inner self was gone, and this fragment floated in nothingness.

Didn't I have anything better to do than ask the price of a Muguet des Bois aromatherapy candle every week to make sure that sixty dollars was what I'd heard? Because my senses were acute, as my friend the recovering heroin addict had pointed out when he said, "You have to develop a protective barrier," and I knew the aroma of the lily of the valley would help me more than a drug. There had to be a way to get some of that fragrance. The dusting powder was what I really wanted and had been searching for since age fifteen, when an inferior, cheap American brand was all that I could find.

Even though Dr. Andrew Weil had warned against the breathing of talc, all brands of dusting powder that I saw, including those from Paris and London, contained that toxic ingredient. Sixty dollars, I'd say to myself, or even out loud, sixty dollars for a candle. I'd say it once a week whenever I passed the store. Maybe I would turn into one of those people who wandered outside stores and said prices into the air.

In the discount drugstore, the woman in black must have seen my loss of the form of a standard human being, and that gave her permission to speak to me. Because before getting into the Dr. Scholl's aisle I'd visited the stationery and school-supply aisle, where I'd picked up a glitter-covered pencil. At first I thought it was pink glitter, but upon closer examination I saw it was a mixture of pink, blue, and white, giving it a lavender cast. The color wouldn't have been so bad if it weren't for the white feather topping the pencil where the eraser should have been. This startled and sickened me at the same time—this feather or feathers, synthetic ostrich feather plumes were what they appeared to be—yet I picked up the glitter-covered feather-topped pencil and studied it for a minute before deciding it wasn't pink enough to bother removing the feather and adding an eraser.

When I paid for the Xanax, the innersoles, and the chocolate, I noticed that the glitter had stuck to my finger and had become embedded in a paper cut I'd glued together with Krazy Glue after hearing Dr. Weil suggest the treatment for cracked heels and fingertips. This was a final blow to the last tiny fragment of self I had dragged to the store that night. The cut, the glue, and the glitter—plus a disappointing conversation with the stock man about the possibilities of other colors of the pencil. This friendly stock man was the only person who'd said a kind word to me that day. The word was "Hello."

I HAD learned not to ask questions of salesclerks when I was in the store of the nearby clothing purveyor I patronized in hopes of finding one white linen shirt among hundreds of unrealistic-looking garments. I had asked for help finding a size. "This is T.J. Maxx—we don't give you no help, you gots to find things yourself," the salesperson said. She said it with indignation, too.

Then the salesperson, a round, dark-haired woman of about forty years and an unknown nationality—this person recognized me from her days as cashier at the discount drugstore. "How've you been?" she asked, or asked in some dialect, like "How you been?" I said fine and inquired as to how she been, and how she had come to be working here instead of there. Perhaps I was more polite and simply stated, "I didn't know you were working here." How could I know? It was the second time I had forced myself to enter the dreaded emporium. I was down to my last two shirts and one had fallen apart as I tried to button it the day before. My finger went through the buttonhole and into the worn-out fabric.

Whenever I'd asked anyone where they'd gotten anything—a plain linen shirt—the answer was always . . . T.J. Maxx. How could there be only that one store serving all the women I asked about their shirts?

They didn't describe how deeply dismal an experience it was

to go into the store. On my first visit I touched fabric that didn't feel like cloth of any kind. I actually touched that, I thought as I looked back at the thing to try to understand what the fabric content might be. It had a slippery feeling, though it wasn't oil-cloth from the 1950s, and no oil had been spilled on it. It must have been woven out of some kind of oil thread.

Then the former drugstore cashier addressed her fellow employee—her colleague who had been chatting with her about a personal matter. She looked at both of us, and I realized with dread that I was about to be discussed by these two, drawn into their circle the way I'd seen a TV show hostess in a middle-of-the-night rerun draw the whole audience into the problem of one crying audience member, or draw the crying audience member into the audience's communal mind: "She fears aging," the hostess had said about the woman.

"She used always to come to the store," the saleswoman said about me. "She's one of the worst chocoholics in town. How come you stopped comin' all of a sudden?"

"I used to bake chocolate cakes for my father," I said. Then I waited a moment while trying to decide whether to add the reason. An obsessive-compulsion made me say it. "He isn't alive anymore," I had to say.

"Oh I'm so sorry," the salesperson said. "Well, may he rest in peace."

But I knew my father couldn't be resting in peace. He'd fallen into the hands of the medical system and had been tortured to death by doctors in hospitals. My unwitting complicity in this, along with that of my siblings, had left me wandering between discount drugstores and all-night supermarkets for the rest of my life so far.

"God bless his soul," the other one said from her place amidst hundreds of shiny synthetic-fabric bras hanging on plastic hangers.

"I used to say, 'How come you're always buying the chocolate and you're still thin?' " the black-haired, large one said. "Now I remember."

I HAD driven away from the drugstore with the rich booty of drugs and soles in a plastic shopping bag—no choice of paper or plastic was offered there—and I knew that the conversation with the woman in black was the highlight of the evening. It was winter and the many hours of coldness and darkness kept down the number of human beings and their huge vehicles. The wide, tree-filled lanes and open fields under the half-moon light were all mine in which to contemplate the emptiness of everything.

The Xanax—I saw how nice and full the bottle was—I'd gone from thirty tablets at a clip to sixty, to ninety, and was now hitting the jackpot with one hundred and twenty. But no congratulatory sticker was handed out or pasted to the bottle the way a sticker was affixed to the windshield of our Volvo when we reached one hundred thousand miles, though I thought I saw that the pharmacist was impressed when he handed me the bag of pills.

Just the sound of the many peach-colored beauties tumbling about and clicking into one another in the newly orange-colored bottle, this made me calm—I didn't have to take a pill or even half of one. The same with the chocolate. I had no plan to ingest any, but just the thought of the big sack full of extra-small-size Hershey bars on sale after Halloween, the vision of the special chocolate-colored, foil-wrapped little bars, prevented withdrawal from the drug I'd read was in the mixture—theobromine. If only that were available by itself.

I'd read in Dr. Andrew Weil's newsletter that those who needed the drug should seek out a good brand of Belgian dark chocolate, or Valrhona, but in a patriotic gesture I never gave up the American brand. Chocolate, a sedative and antidepressant at the same time—except when you think of the nuclear accident at Three Mile Island, which might have caused radioactive contamination at the nearby chocolate factory.

I was planning to spend the rest of the night looking through photographs and slides for my next book, *Look at the Moon*. I was happy to have a night without having to prepare dinner for anyone—washing lettuce, chopping vegetables, the things Michio Kushi writes are good for the soul. But I was tired of the washing and chopping, maybe because I wasn't slicing at the proper angle according to the illustrations in the Kushi Institute's macrobiotic cookbook. And the many bottles of vitamins and supplements on the one chopping table complicated the task.

Lucky for me, my husband stayed in the city all week in order to be near his architectural firm. He, too, was tired of chopping, and liked to order out from a variety of unhygienic food establishments. My last book of photographs included one of him titled "The Man Who Wouldn't Recycle." Another photograph of him was titled "The Stranger." The idea came to me when I told my husband I felt separate from everyone and everything in the world. Without looking up from his crossword puzzle, he'd said, "That's man's fate."

THE BEAUTY ROOM

T HE VISIT to the electrologist/leg waxer right before the trip to the drugstore must have been the event that had worn me down to this low point. I had made it one of my winter goals to be permanently rid of every unwanted hair. I wanted to prevent my eyebrows from growing together in case I fell into a coma. No one had told me how many visits to the electrologist/waxer would be necessary. This is kept secret.

She had been recommended partly on the basis of her owning many pets. But the recommender hadn't said what kind of pets. "Oh, she has animals and birds, and you go to her house, not to a salon in a town," the person had said. "You have to take the ferry to get there, but it's worth the trip. It's neat."

I should know not to take advice of any kind from a grown woman who uses this adjective. And when I got to the house and saw the "pets," I couldn't be enthusiastic. There were about six gray cats walking around from place to place, each cat worse-looking and more sinister than the other. For one thing they were large cats, they were long cats, they moved slowly, staring momentarily at something and continuing on to eat cat food from their bowls or kill something outside. And I thought cats were supposed to be so cute and funny.

I described them to a cat-owning exercise teacher. First she laughed. Then she said, "They must be old, they sound like old cats. They're old cats." Her style was to say things over and over, as if that would make them more true.

"Like what do they do?" she asked.

"They walk from one place to another place and sit back down," I said.

"That's what the old ones are like," she said. She knew about all kinds of animals. Her youngest son owned a lizard and the lizard was always outgrowing his cage. A science homework project at school required something that involved a rat going through a maze. They had a hamster at home, but they'd been told by rodent experts that hamsters wouldn't go through a maze. The exercise teacher and her son had to go out and buy a rat. They asked the pet-store owner whether they could return the rat after the science project. They didn't want a refund, just to be rid of the rat because they had too many animals already. But then they all grew to love the rat.

"The rat was nice and friendly," the exercise teacher said. "He was smart, too."

It was a white rat, and when they approached his cage, he'd come to greet them. When I laughed, she said, "Really, rats are nice, they are, they're nicer than people."

When they brought the rat back to the pet store the proprietor tried to pressure them to keep it. They still didn't want a refund, they wanted only to be relieved of the burden of the care of the rat. The owner tried to scare them by saying snake owners came in to buy rats to give to the reptiles for dinner.

"She did scare us," the exercise teacher said. "We all loved the rat. My son was starting to cry. A teenage girl, a customer, heard the whole thing and said she would take the rat. But when they told her the price of the cage, she couldn't afford it. I said we'd pay half and the store owner offered to pay the other half. The girl was so happy to get the rat. Really, the rat looked so adorable. It was love at first sight."

"It must be the same way women love rats in the human species," I said.

"No," the teacher said. "Rats are nicer, they're not like men."

The only time she seemed happy was when she was talking about animals, the way David Letterman acts when he's on his show talking to dogs.

Lifting weights was boring and we tried to talk about other things. High IQs ran in her family. She had a brother and a sister out west somewhere. I asked what her siblings did, and she said, "Nothing." Her sister worked as a cashier. Her brother was a former juvenile delinquent.

"A tower was named after my grandfather, a mountain was named after my great-grandfather, and my sister works at a 7-Eleven." Further inquiries about the two siblings seemed to distract her from teaching proper form, so we'd change the subject back to the lizard or the cat.

The cat would run away from home for the summer and return in September. She'd vacationed with wealthy summer residents, who fed her salmon steaks or other expensive food. Her fur was thick and shiny and she had a snobby attitude, as if she was doing a favor to the exercise teacher by returning home.

"You would like the lizard," she'd told me on a long, fast walk intended to keep our metabolisms up. "You'd like what he eats. He's a vegetarian. In the morning when I make the kids their lunches for school, I chop up little bits of what I give them— lettuce, cucumbers, carrots, apples. It looks so good. It looks better than people's lunches."

They were supposed to walk the lizard on a leash, to get him some exercise out of the cage. But the lizard was big and ornery—he flapped around out of control and once climbed up a tree and wouldn't come down.

They tried to make an appointment with a lizard-walker specialist because the lizard was five feet long—not even counting the tail. They had to cancel a couple of appointments, then they were embarrassed to ask to make another one. "You know how that is," the exercise teacher said. I said yes. They were at a loss as to what could be done about the lizard and his exercise regimen and he ended up staying in the cage.

THE OLD cats had long and mangy coats of dull fur, and when I saw them I understood what "mangy-looking" really meant. So I'd walk in. But before that—first the ferry ride in darkness, then the drive through dark, wooded roads without any streetlamps or road signs. Then up a winding road to a developed wooded section—the kind where there's a developer's house of every style. Ranch houses from the fifties, cheap pared-down ranch houses from the seventies, Greek Revival columns on shingle styles built in the eighties—and last and worst, combinations of all these styles stuck together on extra-large shingle-style houses built in the last years of the nineties. Fortunately, the electrologist lived in a yellow Victorian house.

We owned an all-wheel-drive Volvo and I could navigate the treacherous, curvy terrain of the uphill driveway and the road on the way to it, all covered with thin sheets of ice under thick snow. Going to the electrologist in all weather was never shown on the Volvo commercial.

"What? You're coming tonight?" the electrologist said on the evening of an ice storm.

I told her about the all-wheel-drive. There was no reply. Just silence.

The skidding of a former Volvo had kept me from important short trips in blizzards. But when two large deer ran in front of the new kind, it stopped without skidding, just as in the television commercial. The right bumper had hit some back part of the deer. I waited and looked out the window to see the animal's condition, but it had scampered off, apparently with only a minor bump. I recovered my wits and normal heartbeat and continued on, just like the commercials with the fun couples on their way to wonderful, snowy activities.

Then, inside the electrology door as fast as I could go, I held my breath as I walked through a hallway that smelled from a mix of a synthetic brand of air freshener and a most gruesome-looking, dark red kind of cat food, which I avoided viewing closely but couldn't avoid seeing in six bowls on the floor. Quickly into the beauty-procedure room, I'd close the door tightly and open both windows an inch.

The electrologist had agreed to this fresh-air allowance but always forgot to open the windows before my appointments. Then, again as fast as possible, to avoid a confrontation with the large mirror on the wall, I'd lie down on the table. Inside the turquoise-blue beauty room—but there was nothing of beauty in there—I saw bottles of nail polish, each a pinker or redder color than the other. They all appeared to have been left over from the 1950s or 1970s.

Everything in the beauty room was disturbing in one way or another, and I closed my eyes the minute I lay down on the table. But most unbearable was the accent of the electrologist—not Queens, not the Bronx, not Brooklyn, but a deadly combination of all three, even though she was from New Jersey. Talking in the accent went on during the waxing and the electrolysis.

During one treatment, she told me that her husband, a retired park ranger, had to help another ranger move some furniture, including some heavy dresses. From the content of the next sentence, I saw that she meant dressers—chests of drawers. This pained me even more than the electric needle between the eyebrows and the hot wax being ripped off the shin, "one of the most sensitive parts of the leg," she said without any expression of sympathy in her so-called voice.

Her other favorite subject was the politics of the Middle East, about which she had strong opinions without having any knowledge of history or current events. The harangue on that subject, combined with the accent and the physical pain, was a new method of torture, in which each kind of pain was increased by the other. This could be a good method for the CIA to use for interrogation, I'd think. It could be justified—"Why, we do it to our own people every day."

In high school, our French teacher had explained with disapproval what caused the American accent and why Americans couldn't learn the French accent. Americans were so lazy and sloppy that their mouths and jaws were lazy, too, and just flopped about the syllables of words. She liked to demonstrate the lazy-American and tight-French jaws to make a point. She was a tiny spinster who had once been young—though I never thought of it then—probably even attractive and young. She still wore a size 6 and let her white hair wave naturally the way it had in the 1930s and 1940s, when this was a style.

But worse than the pain of electric needles, hot wax, and tawdry pronunciation was the handheld mirror. "Here," she said once, suddenly handing me a mirror from a five-and-ten circa 1971. "How do the eyebrows look?"

I was lying down, so I didn't expect the view to be that bad, looking upward, with gravity working in my favor. Still, I thought I'd made it clear that no mirrors were to be handed to me. I took a quick glance. The mirror was large enough for me to see my whole face, neck, and surrounding overstreaked hair. I saw that I didn't look exactly bad, or, really, old—I looked dead.

Where had I seen this look? Somewhere. Then it came to me—it was Marilyn Monroe in a photo I'd seen of her on the autopsy table. A stolen shot that had fallen into the hands, if they can be called hands—claws, paws, or mitts—of *The National Enquirer.*

But I didn't feel flattered by the comparison—even to resemble her in death would be a compliment—it was mostly the whiteness, the paleness, the having given up on everything that was the main core of resemblance.

I handed back the mirror after saying, "Oh God," in as pleasant a way as I could muster up. "Whatever it is, it's fine, I can't see without my glasses anyway." The truth was that her mirror wasn't of high quality and was lacking serious magnification.

Also, there was a bright red inch of skin interfering with seeing the area I was supposed to check for eyebrows.

"Then let's wax your legs," she said. "We did the front yesterday, so we can do the back. There's not much to do," she said, pronouncing the word "there" like the word "yeah." I wondered how much energy it would take to pronounce the letter *r*.

As I started to turn over and caught a glimpse of this form in a large mirror on the wall, I felt that it was no longer only my face that was a pancake-looking thing but my whole outer being.

My white shirt was rumpled and the small shoulder pads had fallen out of place—one too far forward and one too far back. The forward one looked like W. C. Fields's wife's large chest in the movie *It's a Gift,* and the back one added a hunchbacked curve. My hair, face, shirt, and sweater were all the color of pancake batter. I felt my entire being to be nothing more than a flattened-out spoonful of batter waiting to get flipped over to the other side.

And then, when flipped, as I waited for the hot wax to be applied, her two dogs began to bark outside, in back of the house. The barking continued and turned into wolflike howling. In several instances in the past, I had been driven almost insane by howling dogs—the yapping kind, the woofing kind—and early in my career of being driven mad by barking dogs I read that Johnny Carson was suing Sonny Bono over the barking of the not yet congressman's, or even mayor's, dog. There, I'm not the only one, I thought. Even money can't buy peace.

"The wax is too hot," I said to the electrologist.

"It has to be hot or it won't work," she said, but I knew better, having had lukewarm wax applied to my legs in a waxing room in Nantucket. The waxer in the better room blew on the waxing spatula before applying the potion behind the knees and ankles, saying, "How's that, is that good?" over and over in an Irish accent reminiscent of a reading of *Ulysses* or *Under Milk Wood.* "There now, that's not anything, is it? We'll be done right away," she said a few times.

Near my hometown, a hundred miles from New York City, with the wooded yard outside the waxing room where howling beasts were left outside in the cold, I had to save the main complaint for the torture closer at hand, or foot, and put a stop to the burning wax. But the electrologist continued. She had once before insisted that I dip my hand into a bowl of boiling paraffin wax and when I said, "Too hot," she dipped her hand right into the bowl and said, "It has to be hot."

In a subsequent leg waxing trial she asked, "How's the wax?" and when I said, "Better," she admitted it was a different kind of wax. The other kind had to be melted at a higher temperature, but the "beauty-supply company" ran out of the one that melted at the lower temperature. Probably a falsification of the facts by the wax company, and in an attempt to save money an inferior wax had been supplied.

I smelled a cheap-beauty-parlor-perfumed lotion, the kind from the five-and-tens of my childhood, and I asked, "What's that perfume smell?"

"It's just the aloe vera," she said, pronouncing "the" as in the song title "De Boll Weevil."

Then I asked to see it. It was a bright-green plastic bottle of matching green lotion. I knew aloe vera gel to be pure and clear as an icicle. I'd had many experiences with the gel, in addition to the time in Nantucket when my yoga instructor came by with a bottle of aloe vera gel and asked me to put some on her shoulder blades, which she'd accidentally gotten sunburnt.

I showed her my tube of aloe vera, Lily of the Desert. The label read "99% pure aloe vera."

She read aloud the label of her own bottle. " 'Aubrey Organics, one hundred percent aloe vera gel.' I'll always go for that extra one percent," she added, falling forward onto the kitchen table to show the burnt area. She fell onto the table in an exhausted way, acting like Thelma Ritter lying on a bed in an old crime movie when she says to a gangster what I always recalled as, "Go ahead, shoot me. I'm so tired I don't care."

The yoga teacher had never lifted one weight in her life, and she had perfect muscle tone. "Do you walk on your hands three hours a day?" she asked when I commented on her shoulder muscles. The discussion ended in a moment of silent tact.

For three years we'd been at the beginner stage. I'd never thought about walking on my hands, though I was hoping to stand on my head someday, even though I couldn't get it out of my mind that in fifth grade a classmate liked to use this expression: "What do you want me to do, stand on my head and spit nickels?"

When my parents found out about that, in addition to some other things said by the students, our whole family moved to a new town far away and I was transferred to a different school.

In the new town, still in a public school—my parents didn't get the big picture, paying little attention to my education and/or social acquaintances—I heard more crude talk from a sixth-grade classmate who liked to quote her family's housekeeper.

While we were all in love with Elvis Presley, we heard the creepy and freaky Jerry Lee Lewis in the song "Great Balls of Fire." The African-American housekeeper, known then as a live-in maid, had said the sentence to my friends explaining the title.

Since the woman looked like James Brown, I didn't take it seriously, or I took it too seriously and had to dismiss it as the ravings of a jazzed-up, be-bop, oppressed servant. In those days the housekeepers had things like hidden bottles of bourbon in a cabinet, or a son in prison. We knew this from hanging out with them in the kitchen, the way the girl Frankie did in the book *The Member of the Wedding*.

Given the many hours of unsupervised time, without pressure to prepare to attend Smith or Radcliffe, I didn't understand that those in our generation were ever going to grow up. I felt childhood to be a permanent situation for us. During this period of laissez-faire parental guidance, two girls left on their own ate an entire box of Oreos, unaware that the white part included lard as an ingredient.

TO TOP off the evening, after the drugstore visit, I drove to the all-night supermarket. I was afraid I'd encounter a new machine inside, a black indoor-floor-waxing truck covered with splashed dirt and wax. The last time I was there the machine, loud as a bomb, followed me everywhere. I was the only customer.

Outside in the parking lot, I heard an even louder machine. It was a parking-lot-cleaning truck driven in a fast and reckless way in my direction. The drunk or drugged driver was apparently trying to run down anyone he saw.

The organic romaine lettuce area was hard to get to, with a filthy broom always leaning up against the case in front of the organic produce corner. Why was it there? "Let's store the broom here," some employee must have said at an on-location personnel meeting.

Because upon entering the supermarket's cigarette-butt-filled doorway, past overflowing square cement and concrete trash containers, there was a confrontation with the sweepings of gigantic brooms from each aisle, all collected together in front of the entranceway, where the department of bloomed-out and dying flowers had been installed. Dust, dirt, plastic wrappers, soda cans, cellophane, and an everlasting plastic bag on the floor—that was the nighttime greeting.

THE SURPRISE PHONE CALL

W HEN I RETURNED home from this last activity I had squeezed into the busy evening, I was surprised to see on the caller ID that there was a phone call from my twenty-one-year-old friend the recovering heroin addict. The phone number was from his parents' house in California.

I hadn't heard from him for weeks or months. I'd been informed of the addiction only the summer before. After that I couldn't keep track of what he was doing, where he was—in rehab or out, going to classes at the university, working at some job—to use a word I never used but heard in an A&E biography of Mackenzie Phillips during her drug-addiction years, the last time she went to rehab, her sister, or half sister, said, ". . . Okay, whatever."

With this friend of mine, this boy, I had learned to figure: whatever. Whenever he called me, I'd drop everything to talk to him. Not in a social-worker mode, but as a lucky audience for anything he had to say. And maybe it could do him some good, too, now that he was isolated from his addict friends and other friends. He was a lost soul.

I hadn't seen him since his first year of college, four years earlier, and I pictured him as that boy. I didn't imagine him as an addict, since no one had told me that he looked like one. He was living with his parents in their house in Beverly Hills as part of his recovery. During the phone calls of the weeks and months before this, he had complained that he was a prisoner, that they were suspicious of everything he did and said.

I knew his parents. His father was the world-renowned reproductive surgeon Dr. Arnold Loquesto. I'd met the boy ten years before, when I traveled around New England, where they lived at the time, to photograph the eccentric surgeon at his hospital and at home as he ran from place to place shouting out funny sentences.

I couldn't believe my good fortune that the entertaining boy, now known as a young adult, was calling me to talk. To what did I owe this luck? I'd misplaced the collection of fortune-cookie inserts I'd saved in an old wooden bowl after discarding the cookies, so I was in the dark.

I found these inserts so entertaining that I saved them and tried to get more to read and add to the bowl. I asked a waiter in a Chinese restaurant where I could get the fortunes without the cookies, but he didn't understand the question. He and his co-worker laughed and said, "Chinatown." Whatever I was asking about fortune cookies, the answer would be "Chinatown."

I knew I had to get used to people's inability to understand English here in America. But so far I was at the level of John Cleese screaming at the waiter in *Fawlty Towers*. I knew that

Americans aren't permitted the intolerance the English claim as their historical right, and the book *Anger Kills* hadn't helped me yet. I thought fondly of the era during which the question "Do you understand English?" was used as an angry reply in disputes, and wasn't needed for its literal meaning.

THAT NIGHT of the phone call from out of nowhere, he had called to tell me about something that had happened at his job. I'd accepted the fact that he had a crummy job as part of the road to recovery. I didn't know what the Hollywood job market was for recovering drug addicts.

The boy had a job at a company where horror movies were remade. A Hollywood idea—make movies over and ruin whatever was good about them—but we didn't get into that. It was understood. First came the description of the overweight upper-middle-aged office workers. However low their jobs were, his job was lower. He didn't really have a job other than waiting around for them to think of something for him to do.

I interrupted to ask if he'd read the book *Something Happened*, because of its description of office life. I forgot that he'd never read any book I'd recommended, even *A Mother's Kisses*.

He had led me to believe that his mother was hovering over him all the time and watching his every move for no reason. He didn't mention that he was still a heroin addict and that she was watching for signs of that. When I spoke to her she didn't mention it either.

The boy told me that in his job he tried to look busy with any task so that no one would notice him and give him something worse to do. He didn't like being interrupted when I told him about the book. He was driven to continue the line of the story.

When I looked back on this, I thought that maybe he was actually doing a line of coke as he talked.

The workers in the office were interested in candy, he said, and a lot of candy eating went on there. One woman loved the candies Jolly Ranchers.

"Do you know them?" he asked me.

"I've seen them," I said.

Later, on an episode of *The Larry Sanders Show*, I heard Larry's angry joke writer refer to this candy as a kind his friends would search out after smoking dope. If only I'd had the cable channel back when *Larry Sanders* was on TV the first round, I would have had this important clue. The boy had made a tape of a few episodes and sent it to me, but when I learned an additional, large VCR-shaped box would be necessary for transmission, that was the end of the desire to get the cable channel.

I could have had some understanding of lying and cheating and manipulation of people in show business and the entire business world, and this would have helped me in all dealings, since now almost everything in the world is business, other than bird-watching, and this knowledge is a necessity for all transactions.

"Well, she likes the lemon flavor the best, and she buys packs and packs to get the lemons," he said. "Kind of strange, right?"

"Kind of sad," I said as I envisioned the scene.

They threw him old scripts to read; he said they sent him on errands "to deliver headphones, to buy wire in Pasadena." When he said "buy wire in Pasadena" that sounded bad. I could imagine him stopping off to buy drugs when he was out in the wire area of town. It just sounded like it: "buy wire in Pasadena." It had a hard, cruel, and bleak sound.

I knew nothing about Pasadena. I thought I remembered hearing it mentioned in some movies from the 1940s—the one where Barbara Stanwyck is waiting in bed on the phone trying to prevent her murder by a hired killer, or the other one, *D.O.A.*, where Edmond O'Brien ingests a poisonous, radioactive drug that dooms him to twenty-four hours of life, during which he tracks down the mystery of the accidental poisoning, then drops dead in the D.A.'s office or somewhere like that—an office with a wooden door with a glass top panel with names painted on the glass.

Or the other one—*Double Indemnity*—with Barbara Stanwyck and Fred MacMurray, or in the movie version of *I Married a Dead Man,* where two women meet on a train, one is an unwed mother-to-be, the other a happy new bride on the way to meet her husband's aristocratic, wealthy family for the first time. The unwed one—as usual, Barbara Stanwyck—tries on the ring of the lucky wedded one; the train crashes, the newlyweds are killed, Barbara survives with the ring still on her finger and, while unconscious, is presumed by the family to be the new daughter-in-law and is taken in by the mother-in-law, an actress in the style of Ethel Barrymore. She thinks the baby is her new grandchild. Barbara goes along with it.

If Barbara Stanwyck must be watched, I preferred *Christmas in Connecticut.* There, at least, she's in an unrealistically wholesome setup precursing Martha Stewart. That's what I liked best.

But the boy's life was making me think along the path of crime. All these movies came to my mind when he said "Pasadena," and all the cowboy movies I'd turned off when trying to find something on TV in childhood. I thought I'd heard the name "Pasadena," though I might have been wrong and didn't have the will to go out and rent all of them to check. And also I didn't like touching those rented videos that have been handled by others. I'd heard David Letterman say the same thing, so I figured it must be okay. As all these things flicked around my brain, the boy continued with his story.

I asked whether the office workers knew how smart he was. Maybe, he said. It wasn't foremost in their minds. "They don't have minds as you and I know the mind to be," he said.

Did they know what he was doing there? They didn't care. They cared about the candies and the lunches. The best part of his job was taking the lunch orders. At least that provided interesting material and conversation. Later I thought the real reason might have been that he got out of the office and had the chance to buy some drugs.

He continued on. One day it was decided that there would be a sidewalk sale of all the old costumes in the warehouse. But they weren't real costumes; they were polyester garments from the seventies, like thin purple and orange velvet suits with bell-bottom trousers. Also, there weren't any sidewalks.

"It's ridiculous!" he said. "No one lives near us! No one works near us! It's an abandoned lot with a warehouse over some rail-road tracks. There's a bad supermarket down the road and some-one opened an office-supply store near it, thinking customers from the market would go get office supplies, but no one went to the market, so there was no one to go to the office store."

Still, they gave him the job of distributing flyers for the cos-tume sale. They told him to leave some at the supermarket.

"I told them no one goes in there," he said. "They said, 'Do it anyway.' "

At the market, he wasn't allowed to leave many flyers. "They know they have no customers," he said.

I pictured the worst dilapidated markets in vacant neighborhoods I'd gone by in my past. I thought of Key Food stores I'd seen from highways. I felt worse for the boy with this new picture in mind—a square, low, white concrete block with giant red prices on white paper signs in the windows advertising kinds of meat.

"Then they told me, 'Go put them under windshield wipers of whatever cars that are parked.' Don't you think that this is beneath my skills, meager and unhoned as they may be?" he said.

"Way beneath," I said. I wondered whether to interject something about a job I'd had when I was his age. I knew that he didn't want to be interrupted again, but I thought it might help him. In an art gallery where I'd worked as an assistant, I was given the assignment, when the art business was slow, of taking a small gray eraser and erasing the thick white fabric that had been put up as a wall covering instead of wallpaper or paint.

"How big was the eraser?" he asked.

"One inch square."

"How big was the gallery?"

"A great big room," I said.

"But at least it was on Madison Avenue, I bet," he said.

"Yes, but the job was erasing the walls. And I never questioned it."

"You thought it was a good job?" he said.

"No, but I didn't think it was beneath my abilities. The word 'self-esteem' wasn't bandied about at the time."

"My theory is that by the time you're twenty, if you have low self-esteem, you can never get over it," he said with sudden conviction. "I've seen examples of it time and again."

It was a blow to me to hear that. I knew he was right. I must have known it all along, but I needed him to point it out. It was the most obvious thing. I had none—I knew that—but now I understood that I would never get any.

Once, when I described my last attempt at psychotherapy, with an insane psychiatrist, the boy listened, thought for a moment, and said: "He's a crazy man. And you're like a battered woman."

It was a perfect truth. "You're right," I said.

"You make excuses for him and keep going back for more," the boy said as a further deeper truth.

I understood in that instant how I had lost my remaining sliver of soul. I'd seen some news shows about battered women, how they admired the batterers, how they gave up their selves to these batterers. I was just like them.

"When did you realize that wall erasure was a demeaning task, finally?" he asked.

"Never. My closest friend came by to visit. She saw me standing at the wall and erasing it with the tiny eraser. She had to tell me. That night she called and said, 'You have to assert some rights. It's just *common sense* that you shouldn't be standing there and *erasing* the *walls*.' "

Since he seemed interested, I decided to tell more.

"Once I was sent to Saks Fifth Avenue to purchase underwear for the owner's husband. 'I am going to send you on a very personal errandt,' she said with a German accent, even though she was Belgian, or claimed to be. The undershorts for the overweight, blubbery husband were a large size and an expensive price.

"'That was a bad errand, but every few years my friend would still remind me about the erasing of the walls," I told him.

Another errand I'd been sent on was to deliver a piece of sculpture, by subway, over to East End Avenue. Having had a childhood fear and hatred of the subway—the noise alone was a reason—the minute childhood ended I began taking buses, walking, and spending any available funds on taxis.

"The Lexington Avenue line is good, we send our daughter on it," the owner said as she gave me some tokens from an Hermès satchel bag that was high style for grown-up women at the time. These bags didn't impress me one bit. The empty-headed idea seemed to be: a lot of flourish opening the clasp, unbuckling the strap with fluttering manicured fingers, with a sparkly, antique diamond ring flashing around during the opening procedure.

The sculpture was a big, heavy piece of white plaster with melon-size round things attached to the front and back. I took a taxi and paid for it out of those funds of mine.

As I told the boy about these adventures, I became almost ill with the anxiety of remembering the hideousness of my mental condition and living situation at the time. I may have been realizing unconsciously, or in some other manner, that this had been the beginning of the setup for my lack of a soul.

I saw where I was at the moment, listening to his story as the true high point of the evening. I saw that the place of nothingness had gotten into motion during those years—nineteen, twenty—the same stage he was at right then as an on-the-spot participant, and he had diagnosed that there would be no improvement for either of us.

I got a jittery feeling that quickly increased to a panicky feeling, and forgot to do the breathing exercises recommended by Dr. Andrew Weil every possible chance he could. I didn't yet have a woman dancer's book *Healing Mudras: Yoga for Your Hands*, by

Sabrina Mesko, or I could have put my hands on my chest where I felt the quivery, trembly panic originating. Because on the phone and in person people can hear the breathing and misinterpret it, but no one would be able to hear the hand exercises.

"At least you're in your own car and not on a subway," I said to the boy.

"My father's car, but yes, it's better," he said, and continued right along. "I can't believe that they sent you on the subway with sculpture. How expensive was it?"

The boy liked to know the price of everything. He loved money and was already planning a life of great wealth when I met him at age eleven, and probably before. When he was eighteen, he didn't like his cousin's girlfriend acting like "one of those generous kinds of people who are always thinking of giving to and helping others."

I mentioned this quote at a dinner I attended in a Japanese restaurant with the boy's family and the girlfriend. They were surprised. He was absent from the dinner; he was probably in an alley somewhere.

"That's not like him, to say anything good about anyone," his father said.

"He didn't mean it as a compliment," I said in the style called blurting out the truth.

The table full of the boy's relatives started laughing all at once. I saw how good it was to make people laugh—all those faces smiling and laughing. I wished I'd pursued my acting career as a comedienne.

"AND SHE'S a *Beowulf* scholar!" the boy had told me. "She has friends who are members of the Beowulf Club. Can you be-

lieve that? The members receive a *Beowulf* monthly periodical."
When he said "Beowulf Club," I was overtaken by an outburst
of near-hysteria. He knew about this club and he'd been keeping
it to himself.

"See?" he said.

I did see, I told him. I'd given up the required early English
literature course when they got to *Ralph Roister Doister*. Just the
word "Beowulf" brought back a slew of bad memories of the
college experience.

The one thing I'd done that had impressed him was to purchase, at a reduced price, a pale-peach Armani linen jacket I'd
seen at night in a store window in Boston. The jacket had the design of an outdoor parka, hood and all, but the boy didn't have to
know that. I let him think it was as elegant as he wanted it to be.

The only other thing he liked about my situation was my
height. He had a fear of not being tall and as a teenager had
contemplated a new surgical procedure that lengthened the fe-
mur bones by sawing them in half and adding steel extenders. It
could offer a few more inches, up to twelve.

"How many would you do?" I'd asked.

"I'd go for the maximum," he'd said. "While I was at it."

At the time he was five-five, so I said, "Do you want to be six-
three?"

"Might as well," he said. "It couldn't hurt."

"By the way, it must be painful—the postsurgical part," I
said.

"They give you morphine. You don't feel any pain," he'd
said.

JOBS OF YOUTH

Aʙᴏᴜᴛ ᴛᴇɴ ᴛʜᴏᴜsᴀɴᴅ dollars," I said about the price of the sculpture.

"People are like this," he said. "Even more so in that genera-tion. Why didn't they use an art-messenger service?"

"They said it made a better impression to send an assistant."

I remembered myself with youth and looks intact, and my mental state at the time preventing me from knowing I had any of that.

"What were you wearing?" the boy asked. "School clothes like you do now?"

"I wore Marimekko dresses every day, sleeveless in summer and long-sleeved in winter. Do you know what they were?"

I felt more sick and anxious at the thought of the dresses and perhaps having to describe them. I shouldn't have mentioned the word "Marimekko"—the dresses, the era, and the Rolling Stones. The song "Get Off of My Cloud" came into my mind.

Another job I'd had was to work at a Marimekko store in New York for the summer. My job was to rearrange bolts of Marimekko fabric while I climbed up and down a light-colored wood rolling ladder designed for just this purpose. By coincidence that Rolling Stones song was played all day long, and up on the second floor there was no air-conditioning and the heat rose, especially up high on the ladder, where I was often on the verge of fainting.

Later on, I heard that certain male customers took the opportunity to look at our bare legs and even our underpants underneath our short dresses while we were up on the ladder. This was before the present lewd era in which men can see nakedness and underwear right out in public, anywhere, anytime.

"I've heard, a bit," he said nonchalantly. "Some girls I knew in New York told me about the dresses."

"I can't believe they sent you on the subway wearing a Marimekko dress and carrying a ten-thousand-dollar sculpture," my friend, the one who'd objected to the wall erasing, had said at the time. Before that, in a discussion of public transportation, she'd said, "I've never seen a well-dressed woman on the subway."

"What does being well dressed have to do with it?" I asked her. Subway riders could be seen reading *Catch-22* at that time in history. Since she'd been brought up on the Upper East Side, she didn't understand the question. At one time, she confessed, during college, she'd had a drawer filled with Hermès scarves. I'd never heard of Hermès scarves and thought that Greenwich Village was the only place to buy clothing during the college years. I'd never heard of scarf collecting. Later, she gave them all away in a state of growing character development and improved taste.

"So anyway," the boy said, "they decided to haul out all these gigantic wardrobe containers and put them on the street for the sale. You know those cardboard containers that moving companies use for shipping clothes? It's those, but they weigh a ton—they're loaded with velvet capes and boots with metal ornaments. Normally I'm very efficient, but it was time to take the lunch orders, so I attempted to shirk the manual labor. These two women I've endeared myself to were in charge and said, 'Okay, get the lunch, we can handle it.' "

I imagined the boy endearing himself to the women. I was glad that he still had the ability to endear himself to people after becoming an addict and losing his way in life and working as an errand boy at Creative Monsters.

I'd never known any upper-middle-class intellectual addicts. Keith Richards came to mind when the boy's father had first informed me about his son's condition that summer before. I tried to be optimistic and I offered the Rolling Stone as an example of recovery. When I told him that there were success stories and said, "Keith Richards," he said, "Who's Keith Richards?"

How could a person of our generation not know who Keith Richards was? The boy's father knew the whole history of rock and roll and had met Chubby Checker when they were both in high school. He'd also met Fabian, but that was more of a joke.

"The Rolling Stone," I said.

All he'd said was "Oh."

"One of the women had hired a husky assistant for the day of the move," the boy said. "It's not as if it was just the women office workers doing the heavy work, but still, it's a boiling-hot day and they're dragging the wardrobes around and I'm walking out the door to my father's Porsche. I get in the car and I'm driving around the parking lot and this contributes to my looking like a spoiled, lazy brat." He sighed when he said that last sentence. Then he explained, "But it's how I get to work. There's no public transportation."

I asked how his father got to work, where he was dean of a medical school.

"I drop him off. Or I take my mother's Lincoln after dropping her off for some meetings. Anyway, I drive all the way on the freeway packed with traffic, because they all want lunch from California Chicken."

"Aren't they into health food in California?" I asked.

"No, it's just like anywhere else. People are obese and unsightly here, as everywhere in America."

"I thought they had the greatest health food restaurants in California," I said. I was disappointed. I'd heard it since 1969, when health food started in New York. Refugees from California told about sandwiches made entirely of organic vegetables and herbs. One bad thing was the avocado on all these sandwiches.

"They're not interested. Anyway, those places are in the parts of L.A. far from here. I couldn't go there to get the lunch orders."

"By the way, what movies are they remaking?" I asked, trying to get a better picture of the situation.

"*Earth Versus the Spider-Man, War of the Colossal Beasts,*" the boy said without any expression.

I'd never heard of these and I laughed, but not too loud. Just loud enough to lose that jangly feeling of loose metal springs and bolts in the chest. I know laughter is important for health and I'm always forgetting to get some, same with the breathing and the eight glasses of water.

"So I get to the restaurant and there's no place to park. I have to go to private expensive parking—a garage—so I can do the menial delivery. But these two black guys there had pity on my plight and they let me park for five dollars. I said, 'I have to pick up this lunch order for work,' and they thought I was like them, a low-level employee, and they gave me a deal."

The way he said these last sentences gave cause for concern. An extra bonus of elation came creeping in around the words. I imagined him buying drugs from these guys, or getting a tip on where to get some nearby. I knew it and I didn't know it at the same time.

I knew nothing about illegal drugs. I'd never taken any, I didn't go to Hollywood movies, and I turned off the news if it was about that subject. How it's done I didn't know, other than bits of what I'd witnessed in transactions right out in public in Washington Square Park. Sometimes when I had no choice other than walking along the park side, unsavory-looking youths would call out in my direction, "Loose joints." Since I was used to hearing things called out to me and other young women, things like, "Short skirt," "Long hair," "Long legs," "Cool boots," I assumed the unsavory ones were commenting on the way we were walking.

"I get to the restaurant and everyone is well dressed and I'm a delivery boy," he said. "They're giving me glances to that effect."

"How well dressed could people be at a place called California Chicken?" I asked.

"This is what they do in L.A. They have nothing else to do but dressing up and associated chores. Oh, by the way, did I tell you who sat next to my mother and I last week at lunch in Beverly Hills?"

" 'My mother and me,' " I said.

"It sounds wrong—I know it's right. My mother and me. Wait'll you hear this. The one from the murder trial."

"The prosecutor?" I didn't want to think about her face.

"No, you know who, the one with all the plastic surgery," he said.

"That's all of them, I thought."

"No, the worst one. The one who looks like a suntanned monkey," he said.

"Is she an actual person?"

"Yes. It's unbelievable but true. She was with two friends, all with facial work, the kind of women who look like rich men's mistresses. And they were all three on cell phones at the same time."

"Three? I've never seen that," I said. "What were they talking about?"

"Nothing. Appointments for manicures and trainers. One had to go outside to finish the conversation. It sounded like an illegal transaction."

I tried to picture the boy, a person, in a restaurant, sitting next to these caricatures of people.

"So be that as it may," he continued, "I get the lunch after waiting around in embarrassment for half an hour, I pick up the car, and go there and back in an hour. I'm back at the lot, I drive up in the Porsche. They're all sitting outside with the costumes, and not one person has come to buy anything the whole day. One Puerto Rican woman from the neighborhood stopped to look at some things." The hot, dry, dusty poignancy of the scene was getting through to me.

"So I take the lunch in and they're all going through the order with anticipatory glee and this one director who's kind of a pretentious intellectual and a nerd combined but thinks he's great even though look at what he's directing, he's from New Jersey like everyone in California—did I tell you this? When my parents first moved here, I'd tell people I'm from New York and they would say, 'Me, too,' and I'd say, 'Oh, what part of New York?' and they'd say, 'Englewood, New Jersey.' Or, I tell them I live near Gramercy Park and they're like, 'Oh yeah, Greenwich Village. I used to hang out there.' Anyway, this director comes out and sees the staff standing hovering at the lunch order and he says, 'What's this? California Chicken? Why wasn't I informed?'

"They're like, 'Oh, we couldn't find you,' and he says, 'Hmm, well there's something they have there that I really love— rosemary chicken.' "

These two words together always gave me a jolt. One, the green herb, the other, a dead bird—cooked together and served on a plate.

"He has the menu memorized," the boy said. "So after some conference between him and the assistant, he goes back into his office. The assistant comes out and talks to the office-worker captain. Then she comes over and tells me to *go back* and get the omitted *lunch*!

"I tell them, 'There's so much traffic, the parking costs so much, it'll take two hours!' The assistant hears this and walks over and looks at me. Then he says: 'Make it happen.' "

I'd heard the expression, but I hadn't heard it applied to someone's lunch. I thought it was for big-time operations, deals and things of that nature.

The boy had to go back to California Chicken and start all

over. Maybe he saw his life going down the drain with that errand and that day and that trip.

"I always thought I'd be in some important position someday and I'd be saying 'Make it happen,' " he said.

"You will," I said. "But the expression will be over by then."

"It's over now," he said. "Isn't it?"

"I don't even know," I said. "Why don't you write this all down as a story?"

"You do it," he said.

"It's your story. You should do it," I said.

"We should both do it! In a hundred years scholars can be reading them and trying to put the pieces together."

"Why don't you just tape-record all these stories that you've told me since I met you?" I said.

"We should be taping these conversations!" he said with too much sudden enthusiasm. "But I have to get off the phone. I hear my father's footsteps."

"Aren't you allowed to talk to me?" I said.

"They think you're a bad influence."

"I've never even smoked marijuana, or even a regular cigarette," I said.

"It's not you. It's anyone. They don't want me talking to anyone. They want me to be only with them. It's unbearable!"

"Your mother used to ask me to call you every night when you were in high school and they went away to conferences."

"Now they think you're eccentric and antisocial and don't do all the middle-class things they do with their circle of the bourgeoisie. That's actually a compliment. But he's coming. I have to hang up right this minute. Call me on my cell phone later. You can be mulling it over in the meantime. From an existential point of view." Then he hung up.

What I mulled over was why he wasn't allowed to talk to me. I thought of the song "The Bourgeois Blues" and the line "I don't want to be mistreated by no bourgeoisie," even though it didn't apply to this case.

ONLY IN retrospect, when weeks passed and I never heard anything from the boy again, not even an addendum to the story he'd told me that night, and later when his father told me that the boy was back in rehab—this time for cocaine he'd bought on the street in Santa Monica—only then did it occur to me that a drug might have generated the energy for the story.

Never having been out there in Southern California—because, one, it's too sunny and, two, I didn't believe in flying, even before the Event of September—I couldn't picture the scene. I had seen drug transactions on our front steps in Washington Square and all over Greenwich Village when we lived there as a young and ignorant newlywed couple for ten years. We didn't understand that there could be a better place to live than New York City.

I'd seen some intoxicated youths in their vehicles in the supermarket parking lot in Nantucket at one A.M. They were opening cellophane packets of heroin or whatever came in those envelopes. I couldn't be sure, because I always turned off any television documentary explaining it.

I knew there was drug use in California because I'd seen a TV program about Hollywood and most of that program had to do with this subject. Next came a crime show about the drug use of movie stars.

Then one night I noticed that these two shows had been merged, or, quite naturally, had merged themselves into one show called *Hollywood Crime*. I was tired of this show after a second or two, because I couldn't see what was interesting about which actors and rock stars used drugs, were arrested, and were in or out of treatment for their use and so-called crimes. Worse than the facts was the loud, energetic shouting out of it all by the emcee during the entire program.

I couldn't picture a boy for whom I'd child-sat and cooked dinner and with whom I'd watched reruns of *SCTV*—this particular boy—purchasing cocaine in Hollywood. I had to face what a dunce I was. I'd taught him how to steam broccoli, and although he didn't show interest at the time, a year later his cousin told me the boy had asked to have vegetables prepared that way by his mother, who liked to boil things.

YOGA-BALL NIGHT
LAST AUGUST

Our friendship was completely wholesome except for the one night, the summer before this particular winter, the night when we stayed on the phone from eleven P.M. to five A.M. We'd been speaking again for only a few weeks, but as usual one thing led to another. I had tried to hang up at twelve, one, two, three—but he kept talking. This was before his father had informed me that the boy was a heroin addict.

At one point during the conversation I used a foot pump to inflate a yoga ball with the help of the boy's instructions. This took a long time. During the time of the pumping, he told stories of his life in college in New York.

I had diagnosed that lying backward on the gigantic ball would stretch out a muscle spasm in my back. On the other hand, the pain went right through to the chest and was possibly a cardiac symptom. Then, on the third hand, I'd had the exact same thing several times before, a few of them accompanied by normal electrocardiograms.

Either I'd pump up the ball and the exertion would kill me, if the symptom was a heart problem, or I'd pump up the ball and stretch out the muscle and the pain would go away.

I hadn't yet read *Mind over Back Pain,* in which the doctor-author wrote, "narcotics are the best 'pain killers' and the most addictive drugs of people without pain. If heroin were legally available in this country, as it is in England, I would use it in the treatment of patients with acute, severe pain, since it would do the job better than any other legally available drug. This often shocks people, since we have such a strong association of heroin with drug addiction. But any drug can be abused; it . . . happens with heroin so often because the drug is so effective."

When I did read the paragraph, I saw that if I'd been a patient of this back specialist, the boy and I could have been using heroin at the same time—yoga ball and all.

While I pumped up the ball with the foot pump—this by itself was an aerobic workout—I was laughing at a story the boy was telling me about going to buy some groceries at an all-night grocery in New York. His story had to do with the behavior of the cashier.

"Is this you?" she had asked him about the photo on his driver's license. We both found this absurd, and laughed like two lunatics. It never occurred to me that the boy might no longer look like his photo ID.

"What were you buying that you needed ID for?" I asked. I knew he didn't drink or smoke. "I was paying by check," he said. It sounded like a lie.

"She said, 'It doesn't look like you. Is that your signature?' " Then he was asked to sign his name four times.

The security guard, a great big guy, was sitting on top of the ice cream freezer, the boy said with disdain for the low standards of society shown by this behavior. I had seen this style of security and the same sitting-on-freezer behavior in other stores.

"Buying groceries at four A.M.?" the guard had said. Maybe he had the boy's number. The clerks had commented on his purchases, which he said were "comprised of soda and ice pops." Had I known the dietary habits of the addicted, I might have guessed that something was up.

THE NIGHT of that longest call in August, I asked to be excused in order to change phones a few times. I had to tie up the recycling bags, turn out the lights, put my work in order in case I didn't wake up ever again. That had been on my mind since childhood. It was the part of the prayer "If I die before I wake I pray the Lord my soul to take" that had started me thinking.

Then I had to get back on the regular phone, because I'd heard that the electromagnetic field was more dangerous on the cordless ones.

The boy had made himself a cup of tea once or twice during the intermissions, or so he said. When I looked back on it, who knew what he was brewing up.

Maybe it was three or four A.M. when I asked to be excused so I could get ready for bed. I wanted to do all the oral hygiene that went with that. The loud Waterpik—I didn't want to be doing that on the phone, but the boy kept right on talking. He wanted to talk about Waterpiks and toothbrushes and toothpaste. One of his career goals was to start a publication called *Minutiae*. I'd encouraged the project but, as usual with his projects, nothing happened.

Most of the little bit of makeup I'd used had faded or flaked off. I knew how to remove the rest without looking in the mirror, and anyway, I didn't want to see the face of a person who was participating in this phone conversation.

A Pakistani Muslim car-service driver had once told me, "It's good that you don't wear makeup." At the time I wondered what business of his that was. "It's good you wear long skirts," he'd said on another trip, even though half of the bottom half of my leg was visible, though covered by tights.

"When you stay at a hotel, do you bring your own pillow?" the Pakistani driver had asked in a discussion of travel plans.

"Of course," I said, thinking of my buckwheat-hull pillow and a second, smaller one to put over my ear to keep out noise if the sound-blocking machine wasn't powerful enough.

"That's good!" the driver said. "And do you bring your own sheets?"

"I stay at hotels where the sheets are clean," I said. "But I make sure they don't touch my skin."

"Well, you should bring your own sheets, because they don't wash the sheets in hotels," he said.

"But I'm staying at the Ritz-Carlton in Boston," I said.

"When you go to a hotel, *any hotel*, bring everything you can!" he said. "I'm telling you! And bring your own sheets, too!"

During the last two decades of the twentieth century, I had made a study of Islamic fundamentalism just riding in cabs around New York and Boston. This guy and all the other ones I'd met were always approving or disapproving of everything everyone did.

One driver said that blowing up the Fifty-ninth Street Bridge would be equal to what we were doing in Iraq, that time—daily bombing. When I tried to report the information to the FBI after the September event, naturally they weren't interested. The FBI phone operators acted like the telephone information operators who can't spell or listen. Later, when I reviewed these conversations I'd had with Arab drivers, I began thinking more about the FBI and the CIA.

When you called for a radio car, you might get one on time and the driver would follow some kind of rules and procedure. But if any of these guys offered to drive privately, on their days off, anything could happen. They could be an hour or two late. They could tell you their Muslim life stories. They could offer some strong tea they got in a Casablanca-like den of Arabian beverages on a dark and seedy part of MacDougal Street.

Their past lives all over the Middle East seemed to consist of riding camels to property owned by their landlord parents, having lunch, taking naps, waking up for fruit, snacks, cake, and tea. Those were the Iranians. The Pakistani life stories were not as pleasant. A thirty-year-old man had a fifty-year-old mother who couldn't read anything except for the Koran. Her whole life was cooking and reading only that book, he said.

One day, one of these Arabs asked whether I minded if his wife and her aunt rode with us on our trip. He had to take them to the airport and it was right on the way to my destination, where my father lived, or half-lived.

I'd already met the driver's wife on another drive to a non-place in Queens, or Long Island City, where he was dropping her off at a school for medical secretaries. The wife was dressed in the style of Arafat's wife, that unnaturally blond wife with the headband and the speech defect. They were all Europeanized in a style from the past decades—with the Hermès scarves and the

Cartier earrings and the puffed and sprayed hair. The European-ization was never up-to-date with these Arab women.

But on the second drive his wife's aunt was sitting in the car and was wearing one of those black-veil getups. I must admit I was shocked to see this. No warning had been given.

The sight was no more frightening than a nun's black outfit, other than the association of the black-veiled crowds burning the American flag and screaming curses of death against our country.

The aunt appeared to be in her early forties, my age at the time. Her overly dolled-up twenty-five-year-old niece sat be-tween her and the driver.

I was alone in the spacious back of the Lincoln Town Car, so I offered to share the backseat with the wife, who spoke English. It seemed the right thing to do. First they all said no, but then her Westernized mind took over and she hopped out and joined me. Who knew what her aunt and husband were saying in their Arabic language? Perhaps it was simply against some Arab rule.

Somehow, after we started discussing the day's weather, she said she was afraid of the outdoors because of bees. I told her I'd heard that bees like perfume, even perfumed shampoo, and I'd read that one should avoid all scents in order to keep bees at a distance.

"What shampoo do you use?" I asked her. To my surprise she said, "Pantene," as if Pantene were a mark of status like the other products Arabs acquired when their oil money and edu-cational forays took them to Europe. Pantene, originally the French shampoo and conditioner, in demand in the sixties, soon went out of favor and was overtaken by all the new, natural, pure shampoos.

"That's right," she said. "When I was wearing perfume and skin lotions, the bees were buzzing around and biting me." She pronounced the word "biting" as if it were the word "bit," with "-ing" added on. She seemed interested and happy with the information. In addition to bees biting her, at some point she mentioned that she preferred Twinings tea, pronouncing Twinings like "twin," with "-ings"—I didn't correct her. That could be against some rule, too. Not that I thought that our country was innocent of wrongdoing, a country fighting for oil, a country based on cars, driving, highways, gasoline, shopping malls, and junk food. Even though I didn't participate and hadn't yet been inside a McDonald's, I was an ignorant American. But America is a democracy, I'd remember. It was at that time.

This was before they were trying to capture Martha Stewart, who made the right color green available to millions. Just making that color available to the world was an accomplishment, although on some products the green is not quite right, and Martha must have been upset when she saw that.

The black-veiled aunt, silent in the front—this discussion about shampoo in the back—a clash of the cultures right in one's lap on the Expressway. Naturally, I was nervous, especially when the driver remembered he had to return to their apartment to get something for the aunt to take back to their country as a gift for one of those landowning relatives. An argument ensued in part English, part Arabic. I would have appreciated the Buñuelesque quality of the experience if I hadn't been in a hurry to get to my father's house to defrost frozen soup for his dinner.

One night, on a long trip from Connecticut to Boston, the Pakistani driver wanted to stop at McDonald's for coffee. I said

I'd wait in the car. Since I had never been inside a McDonald's, I said, "What's it like in there?"

"You know, like all the others," he said.

"But I've never seen one."

"I can't believe that an American person has never seen McDonald's!" the driver said.

I reminded him about the vegetarian issue. He was one, too. Or he was the kind of Pakistani Muslim who wouldn't eat meat. Then he said, "What about the fries? They are not meat."

"They're cooked in animal fat, I read," I said.

"The fries?" he said. "They are *potatoes,* they are not meat. *Fried potatoes.* They are potatoes."

I knew it was going to be a long explanation. I trimmed it down to a few words he didn't understand.

"I'm going to ask them," he said.

"They're just night workers," I said. "They won't know."

Inside the McDonald's, a chamber of hospital-operating-room lighting and tiles and signs and each thing made to be as unsightly as possible, some ratty-looking teenagers were ahead of us in line. I saw that their hair and their torn clothing marked them as Rastafarians.

The driver looked at them with disapproval. "Why do they want to look so dirty?" he said.

"They're Rastafarians," I said.

"They are punk," he said, his accent making the word sound funnier.

"No, they're Rastafarians," I said, knowing this could start up another lesson.

"No, they are *punk,* they are *punk,*" he said. "I know it."

"Maybe it's a similar style," I said.

.   .   .

WHEN I got into bed and under the thin white blanket, the boy was still talking. That was when I thought there must be something wrong with him.

But maybe a girlfriend had broken up with him and he was practicing up on conversation for the next one. Or he was out of regular friends who were up late. I didn't ask about that. I said, "We should go to sleep."

I know I said, "It's four o'clock." Soon I heard birds start chirping and I said, "It's five o'clock." Once or twice he said, "What? I think I fell asleep for a second."

"Let's hang up," I'd said.

"Wait, one more thing. Tom's toothpaste. What do you know about Tom, the person?"

I told all I knew about Tom. I told about the time we passed through Kennebunkport, Maine, in the seventies, and visited the Tom's of Maine factory, or cabin. At the time, we saw the chemist at work producing peppermint toothpaste and honeysuckle shampoo. Outside the factory/cabin, a teenage hippie was sitting with an unkempt baby in an old carriage.

The boy didn't say anything. Maybe he was sleeping through my telling all this as I was realizing how much time had passed since the 1970s.

I saw that this was what it was going to be like to be the middle generation—explaining why people wore bell-bottoms in the seventies, although I couldn't think of the answer to that, and about the origins of Tom's toothpaste. It was going to be hard for the narcissistic personalities to accept passing out of the young important generation.

THE BOYHOOD PHONE STORIES

W HEN HE WAS eleven, he would answer the phone and sometimes it was a friend of his parents, a divorced or single guy, he wasn't sure which, a guy who wore dark brown gabardine suits with baggy trousers from the forties, the boy said. He wore wide ties with big prints and he wore saddle shoes.

"Some people think he's gay," the boy had said. "But he claims to have had girlfriends. He's up all night watching infomercials for Ron Popeil products. He goes, 'You know that fruit and vegetable dehydrator? I sent that to a girl in Vegas,' or, 'Did you see that Juicerator? I sent that to a girl in L.A.'

"He comes to visit my parents and he follows them wherever they go, to a million parties."

"How does that go over, hanging around with them?" I asked.

"He blends in. No one notices."

The guy in the saddle shoes would call with a medical problem to ask the boy's father. Sometimes it was serious. "Like once he set his chest on fire lighting a candelabra," the boy said. Other times he alluded to his romantic liaisons and had genetic or reproductive schemes to inquire about. "We figure he's not capable of being married, but he wants to sire an heir," the boy explained.

He kept the boy on the phone for hours before asking for either parent. "He calls, I get on the phone with him—it's the peak of sunshine—I hang up, everyone's going to bed."

I imagined the boy's family and household, with his parents and siblings doing different things all day while he stayed on the phone with anyone who called.

But this long yoga-ball call, the summer after college, was different. Because before that summer, the summer of the drug-denial phone call, I hadn't spoken to him for four years. At the time of that conversation, he had moved out of his college dormitory because kids stayed up dyeing their hair purple late at night. He didn't care for the student body, which he described as a motley crew. He didn't like those two new things—multiculturalism and diversity—and had a wish that things were the way they had been in the 1950s. He liked the movie *Rear Window* because of the clothes the actors wore. When he was twelve, he asked me this question: "In the seventies, did people know how they looked, or did they think it was normal?"

His whole life, I realized, was made up of these last two crummy decades. No wonder he was cynical and discouraged by the world and agreed with kids in his generation who were called nihilists and slackers.

As soon as he got to college, he was appreciated by other students and he made friends, but he still wanted his own apartment. He didn't say why. I assumed general misanthropy and a continuing desire to wear neatly pressed khakis and well-ironed shirts. But one of his cousins liked to tell that the boy had insisted on wearing Christian Dior shirts when he was only five. It went back that far.

In high school, in a newly overdeveloped suburb of Boston, he remained the misfit he'd been in childhood. His closest companion was his dog.

"People think I wear the same khakis every day," he'd said when he was twelve. "In reality I have dozens of pairs, all the same." In high school he liked to wear a navy blue sports jacket with the khakis and an oxford shirt, because the jacket had lots of pockets to keep things in and putting things into the pants pockets ruined the straight line.

What things? Keys, wallet, change, pens, pencils—this was before he had the drugs to carry and hide.

"Kids in my school don't even know what a sports jacket is," he'd told me. "One kid asked me, 'Why do you wear a suit to school?' That's how ignorant they are."

"Listen to this," he once said casually during a long phone call during the high-school years. " 'Dear Fellow Student, We regret to inform you that your classmate, __ __, has committed suicide,' " he read.

"Is that true?" I asked.

"Yes. It's a form letter. I get a few every year. It's always the same format."

In his senior year, as he prepared for college, his biggest worry was where he would have his shirts ironed properly.

"Where do you have them done now?" I asked.

"My mother does them."

"What!" I said.

"You think that's wrong?"

"Of course."

"She irons my khakis, too," he said. "And she can't get the crease right."

"Why don't you do it yourself?"

"It's too hard. She likes to do it. It's a privilege for her to iron for her family."

"Where did you pick up this way of thinking?" I asked. "In your Republican conservative clubs?"

"Around. It's everywhere."

I'd had this shirt discussion with him many times.

"You can say, 'Press only, no starch,' " I'd told him.

"I've tried that. We don't have it in the suburbs. The Chinese always starch them. They say okay, no starch, and they come back a stiff board, with a thousand wrinkles ironed into them. The regular dry cleaner just refuses."

The other side of the problem was that sometimes he had to pick up his father's shirts. Wherever they brought them, his father yelled, "Not enough starch!"

"He has us driving all over Massachusetts, and into other states, to get more starch in his shirts. My mother and I both have to do it. We alternate. He opens the box, we're waiting in fear, and he shouts, 'Look at the collar! It's not stiff enough to stay up!' "

Once when we were on the phone during the high school years, I'd heard him say to his father, "No thanks, I'll do it later."

"My mother is away and he wants to know if I have any clothes for him to add to the machine while he's doing his," the boy said. "I'd never let him do my laundry. He's the worst launderer in the world. I'd rather do my things separately than let him mangle and destroy whatever he touches."

"How does he do laundry that it can be so bad?" I asked.

"He uses a thimbleful of soap powder for ten bath towels and fills the machine with an ounce of water. Then he pours in a gallon of bleach. Or he washes a few socks and pours in a whole box of soap. Then I hear him call me, 'Quick, come here! Why are all these suds overflowing?' He has no idea! He puts the shirts in with socks, so the sleeves and socks are tied together and wrapped around each other like a tightly wound rope with a thousand knots. I've had to secretly throw out whole loads of wash he's done.

"He's like one of these cleaning people who don't speak English and put sweaters in the dryer for seven hours on hot. My best sweater—he threw in—I take it out, it wouldn't fit a mouse. I didn't recognize it. I thought it was part of the dog's toy animal."

I IMAGINED the boy in the big house his parents had designed. It was up on a hill and looked like the Guggenheim Museum. But all around it were other houses that didn't look like any museum. The hill was a developer's free-for-all, similar to the one where the electrologist lived, only a more expensive freer-for-all to do anything. The bigness and the mixed bag of architectural details must have contributed to the high prices. People with that money made in the eighties apparently didn't know that the houses weren't built in any known architectural design.

One winter night when I was visiting, the boy took me around the corner to one of these houses. He had a job feeding the fish and the cats when the family was out of town and he had to go over some instructions with them.

"This is the most hideous fish you ever saw," he told me as we walked up the icy hill in the dark. He'd refused to dress for the cold weather—he hated the idea of warm jackets and was wearing his gray Chesterfield overcoat and loafers. Outdoor-weather gear was something he detested, among many other things. "I detest leeks," he'd said while telling a story about the day his cousin had taken him to a restaurant in New York, where he'd ordered a vegetable pie. "I thought there would be the usual number of leeks and I could avoid them, but it was all leeks and I detest leeks. It was an entire pieful of leeks!"

As we walked to the house, he said, about the fish, "It's a huge black tubular body that looks like it's made of rubber from a car tire and it has fangs for teeth."

"Will we see it now?" I asked him.

"Only if the topic comes up in a subtle way," he said. "Don't mention that I told you about it. Don't say anything about anything."

Before we'd left for the rubber-fish house, I'd tried to convince the boy to dress for the weather. After a while, he'd become peeved and then lost patience with the whole project. "It's *fine* to *wear this coat*!" he said. "We're just going across the road." As we crossed, he complained about the cold while his loafers slipped around on the ice. Wearing a scarf or hat would have been demoralizing for him.

"That's what I meant by cold," I said.

"Usually I avoid inclement weather conditions," he said. "I don't have these problems."

We were greeted by a woman wearing a long quilted turquoise-blue-print bathrobe and fluffy royal blue animal-shaped slippers. Which kind of animal, I didn't care to know—I knew I'd seen ears of some kind on the slipper front—rabbit, dog, something for sure. The woman was in her forties, maybe right around my age, I thought, and her hairstyle was this: two red braids down to her waist. Long braids and bangs at this age, to say nothing of the robe and slippers at seven P.M. She had slightly buck teeth and a retainer or some other orthodontic device on the upper teeth.

"Hello," the robed woman said, in that way mothers have of trying to be friendly with odd, silent children and teenagers.

"Hello," the boy said. He introduced me in his awkward style, as if the words were unbearable to speak. It was having to say my name that seemed to be the worst part for him.

I'd been told that the woman had attended a college that had a prestigious dance department. One reason I hadn't been accepted by the college was that no one advised me to express my interest in ballet. No one told me one thing. In fact, my mother wanted to go to antiques stores in the college towns we visited. Antiques hunting was higher on her priority list than the college interview, and I can't blame her for that. In Bennington, Vermont, she'd bought some English yarn for knitting sweaters.

I walked ahead of her, down the Main Street of the town— it looked like the town in the movie *The Stranger*—while I thought about how badly I'd done at the interview.

Later on, I couldn't remember whether I'd been on the waiting list or just plain rejected by the college.

"Children are overrated," my mother liked to say.

THIS IS what can happen to a Bennington graduate, I was thinking as I tried not to look too hard at the woman who could have been my classmate had I mentioned an interest in dance during the interview. She'd given up a career as a harp player to marry and have children with a person with a job in some corporate profession.

The house was chock-full of furniture—all brand-new, dark wood—and upholstery and carpeting in more different bright colors than I could take in. I was getting the jittery feeling, leading to the panicky feeling. I knew I fit nowhere into the worlds encountered when visiting the boy and his family and their friends.

As the woman showed the boy where the cat food was stored, I saw her husband sitting at a new kitchen table in a new kitchen. I tried not to look at the room too carefully. The man looked tired and overworked as he sat there with plates of food in front of him. He had the look of having been beaten down by work and the pressures of corporation life about which I knew nothing until I saw network executives portrayed in *The Larry Sanders Show*.

After making a hasty retreat from the kitchen, I said to the woman, "I understand you have a big fish tank."

"Oh yes, would you like to see it?" she said. The boy looked at me with the look described as "daggers."

We were taken to the fish tank. Around the fish tank were all kinds of other things—expensive art objects, complicated music-listening systems, many-colored glass bowls, glass objects in all shapes, marble things—I couldn't tell what. Marble balls, marble ovals, marble squares, marble, glass, stone, concrete, tile. I began to feel I might faint. Instead, I took some breaths as quietly as possible. I tried to remember the inhale/exhale ratio I'd read about in Dr. Weil's books. Was it four, seven, eight, or seven, eight, four?

"What kind of fish is it?" I asked.

"We have to go," the boy said. "I have homework."

The secret was this: He'd told it to me months before, in a long phone description of his activities. Part of his job was to resuscitate the fish if it stopped breathing. The nature of the fish's physiology and anatomy was that it might stop breathing every day.

"I have to give it artificial respiration," he'd told me. Everything in his life was a bizarre adventure.

He had to check on the fish once a day.

"I have to go over there and see if it's stopped breathing. Then I have to resuscitate it. They showed me how."

He had to put both hands into the tank, catch the fish, and shake it up in some special way.

I asked whether the fish's medical emergency had ever occurred during his watch. He said, "No, they tried to get me to practice once, but I was, like, 'I don't need to practice. I've taken a course in CPR for humans.' If it ever happened, I might just let it suffocate, depending on my mood."

A BETTER adventure for the boy involved what he called "living in the snowbelt." If we had a foot of snow, they had two feet. They were so lucky that it was always snowing in Massachusetts in the winter.

"We live in the snowbelt," he liked to say in a competitive way, even though he didn't like snow. Snow interfered with driving and driving was his favorite activity.

The boy's father was a friend of a professor at Harvard. The boy didn't care for the professor's politics, or his children, because they all went to Harvard and were friends with observant

Jews. "Can you believe kids wear skullcaps around Cambridge?" he'd said. One of these religious, scholarly students asked permission to park her car out in the wide, spacious driveway of the boy's family's house. There was no parking in Cambridge. The car was left there for weeks at a time.

"Several blizzards came and went," the boy said. "The car is buried under ten feet of snow and they decide they need it and they're coming to get it. So I'm home by myself at night expecting the kid to come from Cambridge, I look out my window, and I see six girls in formal evening gowns standing around in the driveway."

"That sounds like a teenage fantasy," I said. "Six girls in gowns appear in your driveway while you're looking out your window one night."

"Maybe, but they weren't that pretty," he said. "A couple were Asian."

"What's wrong with that?" I said.

"I thought in the fantasy they would all look like Grace Kelly."

"Oh," I said. "I see. That again. But how could they be wearing just gowns in the icy weather?"

"They had little sweaters," he said.

I knew the style. But all I could imagine for the gowns was the kind of dress Grace Kelly wore in *Rear Window*, when she's all dressed up and stuck in an apartment with James Stewart in Greenwich Village. "Why didn't you go down to help them?" I asked.

"Well I did, eventually. But first I wanted to see what they would do. I knew where there was a trowel, or some tools and shovels in the garage, but I waited a bit. After a while they knocked on the door and asked for help. I said, 'We might have something in the garage.' "

"Wasn't that cruel?"

"Possibly, but I don't like their old seventies jalopy in our driveway. It's an embarrassment to our cars. And how could they have left it for months of snowstorms and thought they could just come and easily pick it up?"

"Did you help them?"

"No. I stayed up in my room and watched. It was nice enough of me to leave my homework and other activities and go down to the garage and give them the equipment. Don't you think?"

"How long did it take them?"

"They were kind of hysterical. They had a prom or a dance to go to. They were, like, 'Oh no, we'll be late for the prom,' or whatever. They dug for a while and gave up."

"Did you invite them in for some shelter?"

"They didn't ask and I didn't offer. They went back in this one girl's car that they'd come in. Who knows what they did. Now the car is still there, half dug out, half visible in its seventies unsightliness, and a continuing embarrassment to us."

DURING THE early high-school years the boy sounded happy once or twice. One night he answered the phone in a boisterous manner I'd never heard him use. He was calling out in a competitive way to his college-girl babysitter. She had moved in for a week to cook, drive, and be a companion while his parents were away.

"She's really my cousin's girlfriend," he said. "It's not a true business arrangement." He'd already told me a number of descriptions of her, and other girlfriends of boys he knew.

"Isn't her face out of proportion to her body?" he'd said.

"Is it the one with the large chest?" I asked. This was all I could remember other than some extra-good manners.

"These string beans are delicious," I'd heard her say to the boy's mother at a dinner where boiled soft string beans had been served. The beans had turned gray from the method of cooking.

"It's the fault of the guests," the boy's father had said when the boy's mother had announced the condition of the string beans. "They were late. The vegetables overcooked."

"That too," the boy said when I mentioned the chest size. "It's the tiny facial features with the body that's disconcerting. We think a plastic surgeon worked on the face.

"She comes for a week with seventeen sweaters and a bag full of shampoo," he whispered into the phone. "You owe me eight thousand dollars!" he called to her.

"I'm beating her at every game," he said.

"How do you pay each other the debts?" I asked.

"I offered to pay her from my stock account."

"What if you win?"

"She has to iron my shirts," he said.

"Is she willing?"

"She has no choice. I've instructed her on the technique. It's all settled."

I REMEMBERED the early years of my marriage, when I'd taken on the matter of my husband's shirts. My life was a waste at the time. When I attempted to iron one shirt in an emergency and I was caught by a neighbor—not even a feminist—who had come to borrow soap powder or just be annoying about some problem in the dilapidated building, she said, "You iron shirts? Send them out, it doesn't matter. They're covered up by a jacket anyway." I'd never thought of that.

The boy spoke to me about shirt pressing for about half an hour every week until his anxiety reached an intense pitch when his senior year was over. In the end he calmed himself by concluding: "I'll pay some kid to iron them for me."

THE DENIAL

I WAS SURPRISED when he called me in Nantucket in August—the summer of the yoga ball. I'd last heard from him when he was painting his first apartment with his new friends the first semester of college. The boy had practiced talking to his parents' friends his whole life, then he tried out his skills with his peers in college, and he was soon a beloved comrade. But I knew he had a coldhearted streak, too. It was easy to think of any number of reasons he wouldn't want to stay in contact. I'd figured that he had a new life, with friends, even girlfriends, and he didn't need to talk to me anymore, to me or to the guy who watched the Juicerator infomercials.

In a dark and truthful moment, I had realized that I had something in common with that juicerator guy. Because not only did I stay on the phone for hours with the boy but also I had seen parts of those infomercials, too. I'd seen some trampy-looking women waxing their legs with honey wax. One licked her finger and said, "Tastes good, too!" I had to turn off the TV when I saw that.

The guy probably missed out on the infomercial for the mineral powder or powder of minerals that a group of suburban housewives had put together, apparently without benefit of professional acting instructions or commercial-making tips. I was tired when I watched it at three A.M., but I thought I heard the women say, "Gimme that," and, "Lemme see," as they approached one another, attempting natural-sounding conversation about their product. In another infomercial, the spokeswoman was wearing a giant cross on a chain around her neck while she talked about skin rejuvenation.

But the boy acted as if we had never stopped our years of long conversations, and we were soon talking about calendula cream. He mentioned that a gardener was planting flowers near his parents' house. I asked if he'd seen any actual calendula plants growing out there.

"You can make your own skin lotion," I said.

"Oh, I don't need that anymore," he said. "When I came out here my skin turned perfect. I have a bronzed look."

But the all-night conversation was just the warm-up for the next call. "You won't believe this," he said. "My parents think I'm on drugs! And that I've fallen in with a 'fast crowd.' They say I'm a con man and I've conned everyone so I can keep doing drugs."

The unusual combination of drug addict–Republican conservative must have been what he was alluding to. How could my close friend be a Republican? That had been almost as hard to accept as the drug news. I hoped it was a matter of wardrobe and grooming that he liked and the stage would pass.

At the time of the drug-denial phone call, he was staying with his parents in Beverly Hills. He said that they had dragged him back there, where he was being kept under surveillance and subjected to indignities involved with drug testing. "They think I've tampered with the specimen. Can you believe that?"

I didn't know about drug testing. How it's done, this was news to me. Why did I have to know? The situation had never cropped up with anyone I knew. All those TV programs about watching your children for signs of drug use were shows I could turn off. One reason I had postponed having children was the fear that they would become teenagers and start to smoke cigarettes. I didn't envision tattoos, piercing, rap music, alcohol, and drugs. Too much thinking didn't always pan out.

"Think a million times before giving birth." I'd read that quote, or something like it, in an article about Louise Nevelson. Even with all the mascara the famous artist was wearing in the photo, I took the idea seriously. She had put her work first and neglected to give her son enough attention. He became embittered, and they were estranged for a long time. Late in life, they had a reconciliation. A stormy and tormented relationship could be read between the lines.

When I called the boy back the next day, his mother answered. She was cagey in every sentence.

"We have reason to be suspicious," she said. "Did he tell you why?"

I told her that he had mentioned his weight loss and the fast crowd they thought he hung out with. "Everyone in my family's overweight," he'd said. "They have no idea of normal weight."

"Did he tell you the other part?" she asked.

"He said he wasn't using drugs. That's all."

"We have evidence," she said.

"What kind of evidence?" I asked. I pictured needles and packets.

"I can't speak about it," she said. "This is a problem within our family. I have to go pick up the dry cleaning," she added, and hung up.

The boy called the next day. "What evidence? They found matches and a lighter in my apartment in New York."

"What was all that doing there?"

"Some of my friends smoke," he said.

"You allow smoking in your home?" I said.

"Eighty percent of the kids in New York smoke." It was a made-up statistic, I could tell.

"Why don't you go to some rehab place?" I said. "That will settle the matter, or if you need help, you could get some."

"I'm not using drugs!" he said. "It's ridiculous! I've already gone with my parents to a clinic. They did tests and told my parents I'm not addicted. But still, they won't let me go back to New York. I have nothing productive to do here."

The next day he called and said, "Did you tell my parents I should go to rehab? They burst into my room this morning. They woke me up at nine A.M. and said, 'So you want to go to rehab?' "

"I suggested it would answer the question," I said.

"Don't mention the word! Did you tell them I had connections in New York?"

"I said 'friends and connections' as your reason for wanting to be there. That's what you told me."

"Don't say the word 'connections' to them!" he said. "My parents are behaving like paranoid imbeciles! I have a plane ticket.

I'm going to run away, back to New York. And now I really am going to change my name."

Since he was eleven, from time to time he would say, "I've always hated my name." One name he was considering was "Rick Logan."

"What do you think?" he asked.

"It sounds like a private detective," I said.

"I thought of that, too."

"And it's an airport."

"Does that matter? You think it's not a good association?"

"Not that good," I said.

THE EVIDENCE

A ROUND LABOR DAY weekend, there was a message from his mother on my answering machine. The message concerned the boy's whereabouts. "We're on a plane to New York. We were wondering whether you know where he is. We can't find him."

When I called her back on her cell phone, she said, "He's with us. We'll talk to you later. We have to go get something at the deli."

When I spoke to him a few days later, he told me he'd unplugged his phone so he could get some sleep. Otherwise his parents were calling him every five minutes to check up on him. "They thought I'd run away to stay with you," he said. "They're preposterous in every way."

I imagined him showing up on the doorstep. It wasn't even our own doorstep. The step was in between lavender and roses and pots of white flowers. I didn't see a heroin addict sitting there. Though a man was found drunk and weeping on the curb the year before, while we were in the light pink kitchen cleaning corn.

The apprentice summer police came on bicycles and questioned the man. He had just flown in from New York, he said. We couldn't avoid hearing the conversation, with the windows wide open in August. He had been given alcoholic beverages on the plane. He was on his way to a benefit for a disease and his friend had died of the disease. He kept crying.

I put the corn down as I overheard the man's story. I stared at the corn silk. It didn't seem right to sit down and eat corn. But my husband would expect to have dinner no matter what story was being told outside on the curb.

I HAD invited the boy to visit a few times the summer before he started college, and he pretended he might accept the invitation. When he was living with his parents in Boston, it was so close he could take the fast ferry and come for the day. What else did he have to do? He had no friends. His parents were away. He drove around trying to get his shirts pressed, buying soda, ordering pizza, reading philosophy, history, and the Bible, calling commands to his dog, and talking on the phone to anyone who called. On one occasion he read me an excerpt about Moses. I was so surprised by the subject and his earnest reading of it that I forgot to listen to the content.

When he was in high school and his parents were away on a trip, he'd been sent to stay with some friends of theirs for a few days.

"I'm put into a ruffled room," he'd said. "Everything in the room is Ralph Laurenized. The sheets are new and stiff with a chemical coating. They're all flowered and matching everything in the room. The husband comes home from work and takes off his jacket and puts on a gray sweatshirt over his starched white shirt and blue striped tie. Does that make sense? Shouldn't he take off the tie? The tie is the uncomfortable part. Then they each have their own TV and lounge chair in different rooms, separated by a hallway. They both sit down and watch different news programs. They call across the hall and tell each other what's on the program."

I asked what he had done while the couple watched their programs.

"I stayed in the ruffled room," he said. "There was a TV, but I listened to Mel Tormé on my Walkman and I read."

I told him he'd have his own little guest cottage with central air-conditioning and he'd never have to see us in between activities. On second thought, what would the activities be? He didn't like the outdoors except as a means of getting back indoors someplace else. I never saw or heard about a bicycle. Swimming, sailing, biking, hiking, berry picking—these were alien to him.

I wouldn't have any idea of what to do with a recovering drug addict. I could be duped.

THE MISSED BOAT

A FTER THE DELI and airplane phone calls, I waited a day or two and called the boy's parents in California. It was the end of Labor Day weekend.

"We found him back in his apartment. He was on drugs," his father said. The phrase "on drugs" had a quaint and dramatic sound.

They took him somewhere, or to a couple of different somewheres—a hospital, a clinic—he wouldn't stay, the boy was a legal adult, they couldn't force him.

"You missed the boat on this," his father said to me.

"I'm the one who said to go to rehab."

He ignored that and continued, "A young man you know, and speak to frequently, and consider to be a close friend . . ."

I repeated my sentence. The word "rehab" was like a joke, something I'd heard on *Hollywood Crime* and A&E biographies.

I couldn't believe that was in my vocabulary and that I had to say the word every day.

BEFORE SEPTEMBER, I still thought the substance in question was cocaine. The boy was awake all night talking, and that was the one sign I knew. An actor I knew told me that he'd tried the drug. He had to stay up all night, he wasn't hungry, there was nothing to do. Talking was out, since actors don't have much to talk about other than themselves. When Alfred Hitchcock said actors weren't intelligent, he must have had this in mind.

During the night of the all-night call in August, the boy described the newest psychiatrist he'd gone to. He'd wanted to go to a Freudian, but the prominent Freudian he'd been sent to for consultation was one who wouldn't take on his case.

It turned out the Freudian was the same one I'd been sent to twenty years before and he didn't take on any new cases. He was a short, chunky German with a valuable art collection in his ten-room apartment-office on the Upper East Side. He was the kind who was pleased with all this. His racket was: He listened for one appointment; it was a short appointment, too. He said a few sentences in the blunt-style German accent, charged a high fee, and sent the patient on to someone else; he didn't care what the outcome would be. The boy was sent on.

He described the next one. "You go in, he doesn't have a desk, you both sit at a table. The table is high—it comes up to your chest and neck so it's just these two heads suspended."

I started to laugh, I was laughing like a madwoman, but he continued on in a low voice without joining in the laughter.

He didn't mind going to any of the appointments. It was an amusing experiment for him no matter what the diagnosis was.

"According to them I have hypomania," he said. We both laughed at that. Just the word. It was new.

"I don't know any way to find a good psychiatrist," I said.

"That's because most of the population isn't intelligent," he said. "And these people are drawn from the same pool."

When he said "the same pool," it made me laugh again. It must have been my desperate state of nothingness that caused me to laugh like that. Maybe I had hypomania, too.

"I'd ask for a recommendation for you, but the one I know is too out of it to ask anything," I said.

"You still go there?" he said with renewed interest. "I can't believe you would ever go there again."

"His grammar is perfect. He doesn't have a New York accent."

"I think you should get a dog. I've always told you that," he said.

I'd read in one of Andrew Weil's books that he told his problems to his dogs and this was more helpful than years of psychotherapy. The boy was in agreement without saying so, because he disliked Dr. Weil's wide white beard.

"But I like cats," I said. This was before I'd seen them hunt small birds.

"What can a cat do?" he'd said the first time this came up, when he was twelve. "A dog, you can have an understanding with. They're never in a bad mood. They don't get angry. You can throw a ball"—he stopped when he realized that sounded like a normal human activity in which he wouldn't want to be seen participating—"Oh, never mind. Get a cat. But it won't be the same."

We had given up the topic, but now it was back. "You're allergic to cats," he said. "And I advise you not to go back to this guy. He's completely unprofessional."

"Why don't you become an analyst?" I said. "You're so good at it."

"I'd like to. How much money do they make?"

"Not as much as investment bankers," I said.

"Do you have to go to medical school?" he asked.

"No, you can be the other kind."

"Which makes the most money?" he asked.

"It's all up in the air," I said. "Anyone can do anything now, as you've seen for yourself."

"I'd have to have a very select group of patients and see just a few," he said.

"But you don't like people," I said.

"You think that would get in the way?" he asked. "Couldn't I keep it hidden?"

SKIN TALK

W ITH HIS FIRST girlfriend I knew about, in his last year
of high school, the relationship had a lot to do with skin medications. He said they would meet for tea in restaurants in shopping
malls around suburbs of Boston and they'd discuss remedies
they'd tried. They might have discussed other topics, too, but
that was one he told me about. Maybe she introduced him to
cocaine—not just skin medication. I read him the quote from
Andrew Weil's book about using calendula lotion made from
marigold petals. Later on, when I asked if he'd tried it, he said,
"Those petals?"

"No, the cream manufactured from them," I said, trying to
get him to see it as a scientific product. "You don't use the petals." I thought about all the women and girls I knew who would
have liked to use flower petals every way possible, but now I was
talking to a boy. I wasn't used to that.

"I use hydrocortisone for everything," he said. "It works."

I read him another quote from Dr. Weil's book: "Even topical steroids are dangerous. . . . All of these products are absorbed through the skin . . . and can suppress activity of the thymus, the lymph nodes and the white blood cells." Because he disliked Dr. Weil's beard he paid no attention.

THE BOY said the restaurant where they met was in what sounded like "Foucault."

"What's that?" I said.

"A food court," he said. He described what it was.

I asked how he could go to a place called that.

"Convenience," he said.

"Why don't you go to Cambridge for tea?" I asked.

"Too grungy, and too far away," he said.

I told him about what Cambridge was like when I lived there in the sixties. I asked if the Bick was still in Harvard Square, and he said, "What's that, the Bick?"

I said, "The Hayes-Bickford. There was only Lipton tea at the time. Earl Grey was just beginning." The boy loved Earl Grey tea and asked for it whenever he went out for dinner. "But there were reported sightings of Bob Dylan and Joan Baez in the Bick," I said.

"They both sicken me," the boy said. "Especially him."

Since I'd known him, his musical idol had been Mel Tormé. By the summer of the long calls he had stopped talking about Mel Tormé.

"Well, they're not hanging out there now," I said, referring to Joan Baez and Bob Dylan.

"Oh, you don't know what it's like now," he said. "It's like anywhere else."

"It was already ruined when I was there in 1976. Harvard Square was getting to be like Washington Square, and Brattle Street was almost like Eighth Street."

"Every part is bad now," he said. "The whole world is ruined."

THE YEAR OF REHABILITATION

D URING THE YEAR, starting from the discovery of the drug addiction, whenever I called him at his parents' house, his mother would say, "He's out with friends," "He's doing an errand," "We're going to a black-tie event."

One day she said nothing and called the boy's father to the phone.

"He's in rehab for heroin addiction," his father said, without any warm-up. It was hard to think of my formerly little friend in connection with the word "heroin."

He'd already been in and out of some short programs, his father said, now he'd be in for a week. I knew from the A&E biographies that a month or six months was the rule.

According to reports, which came every now and then from his father, he'd been rehabilitated. He had a job. He was looking for a job. He was taking a class on this coast or that, or even going to London. I believed all this could be possible.

I'd had the idea that if he went back to live in New York, he could go out to dinner with my husband during the week. But I knew the boy disapproved of my husband's shirt-wearing habits. Once he'd come by the apartment and he'd seen some clothing set out on a chair for the next day. The blue oxford shirt was a new one from Brooks Brothers, still in the plastic bag, with pins from the factory, or their own workrooms, as the company's ads read.

"Does he wear the shirt right out of the bag?" the boy had asked. "He doesn't have it washed and ironed first?"

"Is that what you do?" I asked.

"Yes. They're all creased in there," he said, trying to make sense of the sight. "I can't believe he goes to work at an architecture firm in New York in that."

WHEN HE was in L.A., it seemed that the boy had no life other than proving he wasn't an addict. He would be set free to resume his life in New York after he'd proved this. He did imitations of his parents' discussions about him. In the past, his foreign accents—French, Swedish, Pakistani—were among his many talents.

He said that his mother had found a vitamin pill on the kitchen floor in his apartment in New York and whispered to his father, "We don't know what this is." The boy said the sentence in the voice of Rick Moranis as Merv Griffin on *SCTV*. "It's a vitamin B complex. My father, being a doctor in the medical establishment, doesn't believe in vitamins. They're having it tested to see what it is. Can you believe that? Then, at dinner, they're always watching every move I make. I'm under constant observation—my father looked at my eyes last night and asked my mother, 'Have his eyes always been so squinty?' "

In the past, the boy had attributed his eye shape and bone structure to a Mongolian ancestor and this didn't bother him.

When he was twelve and I'd mentioned that Senator Joseph Lieberman resembled Alfred E. Neuman, he said without any expression, "I've been told that I look like Alfred E. Neuman." He didn't seem to mind. Maybe he was already cut off from normal human emotions.

When he outgrew the Alfred E. Neuman stage, he began to look like the actor Jeff Chandler. Gradually it came to me: everyone in the family looked like Jeff Chandler—these were his mother's genes—or a chubby version of Lyle Lovett—his father's genes. The offspring had the combination of Jeff Chandler and Lyle Lovett—the mixing up of the chromosomes and coming up with something in between. I asked the boy's father what the word was for that. He said the word was "syngamy." I told him my reasoning.

"Jeff Chandler and Lyle Lovett!" he said. He wasn't at all insulted.

"What makes them suspicious about your eyes?" I asked the boy.

"Who knows? I can't help my eye shape," he said. "Then they want to know why they never meet my friends. Why I don't have girlfriends to the house. It's because I don't want my friends to know my family background and behavior. It would hinder my social progress."

BACK TO NEW YORK

Somehow, sometime in September, they let him go back to New York. But his mother went with him—it was a foible of their distorted thinking he had to tolerate, he said. He was forced to move to a different apartment, and his mother had set herself the job of organizing his possessions.

When he called me, always in secret from his cell phone, he said he was trying to escape the clatter of pots and pans she was unpacking in the small kitchen, the kind of kitchen kids in his generation were cursed with at the time. I knew of one student on the Lower East Side who had a bathtub in his kitchen. But that was considered good, not bad. Most kids were living in tiny dungeons without any tubs at all.

My friend, this boy, now lived in something that had once been a building.

He had moved out of his college apartment into a better apartment for graduate school but ended up going to rehab instead. After that, he had no choice other than to move into a small apartment his parents kept in New York.

I had walked him back to this place when he was staying there, his first semester of college, the night he viewed my husband's shirt. The apartments, as well as the whole interior of the building, had been ripped out and a warren of cells had been put in—constructed or something less than constructed—and rented as apartments. The lobby—I couldn't describe that, or the elevator, because it was dark gray and lumpy, with mirrors everywhere, and I had to wear tinted glasses and keep my eyes on something else in order to avoid seeing it too clearly.

The elevator in our old building—yes, graffiti on the walls, including the f-word and a series of swastikas, but at least the elevator walls were wood and the halls were plaster. I didn't recognize the building materials used in the boy's unfortunate new dwelling. They were all fake something, I couldn't tell what— maybe cement or concrete. And the narrow, dark hallways, with everything painted dark gray—it looked like a prison I'd seen in a documentary about prisons in countries I'd never heard of.

"What's your mother doing there?" I asked.

"Who knows. They think I can't do anything for myself anymore."

"But you lived alone those four years in college. You graduated and were accepted into graduate school."

"It's unbelievable," he said.

Then I asked, as I'd done many times before, "Have you read the book *A Mother's Kisses*?" I thought I'd sent it to him a couple of times by then, until it was out of print for a while and then reissued as a paperback with an especially bad and unrelated cover. When I saw the cover, I sent the book back to the bookstore with instructions to notify the publisher that the cover was the reason for the return.

The important part was that he hadn't read the book, or any book I'd recommended. And he'd tricked me into thinking his mother was just like that other boy's mother. I wanted to know why our conversations were secret. If his mother answered the phone, she'd tell me about how she was unpacking.

"She's reorganizing my medicine chest in a way I can't find anything," he said. I figured he meant things like shaving cream and toothpaste.

I didn't know that people in that condition were organized by parents, as if starting college or camp, and then left alone to fend for themselves. Alone in New York, no school, no job, friends all dispersed to graduate school elsewhere.

"When is she leaving?" I'd ask him. No one mentioned that he was a heroin-wrecked invalid.

"Any day now, I hope," he'd say, always sotto voce. Then sometimes a sentence would be called into the other room, or roomette, as the apartment didn't have rooms as we know them to be. "Mom, where'd you put that razor Dad gave me?" or "Where's the cereal box from Healthy Pleasures?"

THEN SHE was gone, but in a few days she was back. Still, no one told me what was happening. What is the life of a recovering addict? I should have read up on it, but it was too sordid to think about the boy in this way.

From September through October, I had a sick feeling. I was naturally sickened by the thought of New York City, especially in the permanently hot fall weather. Then there was the thought of a new generation of young people trying to live there—this young person in particular in that dank cell block without any life structure.

TEA PARTY

AFTER HIS MOTHER left, he settled into some form of life. He'd sound tired or sleepy, or way up, as on the night his close friend came to call. It was eleven-thirty or so. His phone had been busy the whole hour before. He had on his happiest voice and tone. This must be the origin of the word "up" when used in drug parlance.

"I can't talk because a friend is coming over. She'll be here any minute," he said.

In my naïve manner, I assumed it was a friend or a girlfriend. Underneath, I may have known that wasn't likely.

He asked, "What's happening?" I gave a brief run-through of my condition of emptiness.

"My friend who's coming over has the same kind of problems as you do," he said.

"How could a friend of yours have the same kind of problems I have?" I asked. "How old is she?"

"Forty-nine," he said.

That made me laugh. Then I said, "How could a forty-nine-year-old woman be coming over at midnight?"

"We have tea and we talk," he said. "We discuss her problems."

"For how long?"

"Sometimes all night," he said.

"Is she married, or what?" I asked.

"She lives with a guy who's mean to her. Sometimes he comes over, too. Then he leaves and she and I talk. She never sleeps at night. They're free to call me at any hour, and I, them." The construction "I, them" startled me.

"What does she do in the daytime?"

"Nothing. She used to be in the film business in L.A.," he said.

That was a tip-off. But it didn't tip me off.

When I thought about the visit from the forty-nine-year-old friend, the visit didn't seem right. Her name sounded like a made-up name. The boy sounded too happy when I heard him greet the forty-nine-year-old guest and her fifty-five-year-old boyfriend while he was still talking to me on the cordless phone.

What could be so exciting about such a visit? I knew how much fun it was to talk to this boy, and I figured these could be two more similar cases, like the guy who set his chest on fire, and me—this was the most fun in their lives, or our lives, but what about the boy, what was he doing with these people?

The next time we spoke I asked him. He said that the man was in the building-contracting business—a bad sign, I thought. He'd escorted the woman to the boy's apartment and soon left.

In retrospect, a drug scenario was the only one that made sense. They were hands-on dealers. Maybe the boyfriend obtained the drugs, then this forty-nine-year-old woman stayed with the customer and they used some drugs together. This made me remember a similar story in the *Enquirer* about John Belushi's drug dealer.

When I mentioned John Belushi's case to the boy later on, after his situation was out in the open, I asked, "Didn't you think it was dangerous?"

"I had a reliable source," he said.

Then I said, "If John Belushi and Janis Joplin didn't have a reliable source, how could you?" I knew he didn't like, or detested, Jimi Hendrix, so I left him out. When he didn't have an answer, I said, "If you're thinking of doing this again, you should go to England, where it's legal and safely administered. That's what Marianne Faithfull did."

"Who's Marianne Faithfull?" he said without interest. "Some ex-hippie?"

BUT AT the time, that fall, I could feel only envy at the thought of what the boy had me believe was an all-night tea party. I could always drum up a feeling of inferiority to his new friend. He said that she looked like she came from Connecticut, whatever he thought that meant. It wasn't the looks I felt inferior about. It was the admiration in his voice when he talked about her.

He liked everyone to look like the models I remembered in the Rheingold girls contest from the 1950s. Six models who looked almost exactly alike were photographed for a small, standing cardboard poster, and customers at grocery stores could vote for whichever one they chose. When I asked my mother which one she would vote for, she said, "None. They all have a flat look."

I reminded the boy that the 1950s were over and all kinds of people lived in Connecticut now, even New Canaan. "David Letterman lives in New Canaan," I said.

I reminded him that he himself was from Massachusetts, equal or superior as a state, and had lived there his whole life until he went to college in New York.

"But she's from Fairfield or Darien," he said. "Where we lived was near Cambridge. It was different. Professors, doctors, Jews, Indians, everything."

"That sounds better to me," I said.

"People from her background have a smoother path in life," he said.

"How do you mean?" I asked.

"It seems less comical."

I'd call every few days, then give up for a while. It was easier to imagine he had the friends than to think he was smoking heroin from a pipe. I didn't even know it could be smoked. Later, when his father told me about the boy's smoking of heroin, I could only picture a small black licorice pipe that children play with and then eat.

THE BLANK SPACE

AFTER A FEW WEEKS I called his father, or mother—whoever answered the phone. He was back with them in Los Angeles. Something had happened. They didn't say what. They summed it up—he couldn't take care of himself, get it together to have meals, and go to a job or to school. He had to live with them for a while.

The period of blank space began—the space of not knowing. He was going to take some classes or he was getting a job. But somehow as the time passed, he never took the classes or started any job.

One day when I called, his father said, "He bought some cocaine in Santa Monica."

It turned out that the boy didn't want to go to the most highly recommended rehab place, in Arizona. He wouldn't say why. When I'd told him about it before, he'd said, "They give everyone a horse."

"How do you mean, to take care of?" I said.

"Right, to take care of," he said.

"I'm sure they don't force you to have a horse," I said. "You could have a dog instead."

"I don't think so. I've met kids at other rehabs who've been there," he said. "It has to be a horse."

He was permitted to choose the place he wanted to attend. When I heard the name of the place, in or near Los Angeles, it sounded like a TV show, a Hollywood movie, or a deodorant.

"That's what he wanted, so that's where he is," his father told me.

"Can they get phone calls from the outside?" I asked.

"I don't know. I'll ask him," his father said. I knew that meant I'd never hear the answer. "I'll ask" was a technique the busy dean of the medical school had learned in order to get rid of people and their questions.

"You must feel relieved," I said. I assumed in my ignorant way that the addict goes to the place, the addict is safe, worries are over for a time.

"Yes, relieved that we don't have to be watching him," his father said.

Later on, I found out that some recovering addicts don't even like the rehabs and even commit suicide while in these places. But back in my ignorant state, I was relieved, too. I pictured the boy in groups where he was given substitute drugs.

When I asked his father how the stay was going, he said, "Good. He asked for some things—books, a shirt."

"Which books?" I asked. I didn't ask about the shirt. The boy who'd been so fastidious about shirt pressing was now in a place where he had to ask for clothes from home. Probably the other inmates wore T-shirts, T-shirts with writing and names of things on them.

The boy and I had discussed how much we couldn't stand that. I had to turn off the David Letterman show when he sent the camera outside to film the people on the streets, people with T-shirts hanging out of shorts—overweight big-legged people in sneakers—all this in color. The Groucho Marx audience of my childhood in black and white was so much more pleasant to see. Polite, repressed grown-ups in suits, hats, gloves—everything I disliked at the time.

I pictured my friend in a circle of addicts dressed in those kinds of T-shirts. I thought that it must be like a prison where the inmates exchange and share bad new habits.

I hoped he had a private room, although he'd started out well in college, tolerating strange dormitory living conditions during orientation, where students of all ages, from many different departments, were thrown together haphazardly as roommates. His temporary college roommate was a forty-four-year-old Swedish photographer who dressed all in black—black turtleneck, jacket, chinos, shoes, and socks. The roommate would come back to the room late at night with noisy parcels crunching into one another. The boy told me, "He apologizes and says, 'Presents for the wife.' " This was the first time I heard the boy do his Swedish accent.

When he returned home and I asked about the rehab place, he said, "Oh, I don't want to talk about that." It was the first time I'd heard him speak in a new, dark voice.

In the next conversation, I asked, "Did you at least meet anyone interesting there?"

"A few," he said. He met some movie stars I'd never heard of. He named their movies and TV programs. I'd never heard of those, either. He named a girl who was the daughter of some singer I'd never heard of. I asked what her addiction was and he said, "Marijuana." She'd already been to that place in Arizona, he said, but I was unable to keep my mind on all these different addicts, their drug habits, and their rehab experiences.

I SETTLED into accepting that I couldn't know what the boy's life really was. *Boys' Life*, I remembered, was the name of an antique magazine or a book. Those boys, Boy Scouts and such, were shown in the book or magazine rubbing sticks together to build campfires outdoors. The boys participated in every kind of wholesome outdoor activity, unlike the boy I knew, whose favorite outdoor activity was driving.

When he'd gotten his driver's license in high school, he was as happy as possible—for him. He described going for a "nice crisp drive" in his father's car around the Wellesley suburbs. I said that the word "crisp" referred to walking—a walk on a crisp fall day. His reply: He kept the sunroof open, or the windows open an inch or two, before he got up to the main road.

WHEN HE was twelve or thirteen, his parents had insisted he do something for the summer with other kids his age. "They're making me have a part in *Brigadoon*," he said. It was an amateur production in a kind of theater camp. I didn't know *Brigadoon* and lumped it in with other musicals I didn't care about.

The production was going on right near New Haven, and on his lunch hour he'd walk into New Haven and go to a used-book store. "The owner is an ex-hippie," he said. "The kind with a gray ponytail."

"I can't stand that," I said.

"Me neither. But he's not the worst of that ilk, he's not as slovenly as some. He's suspicious of me, he watches me the whole time. He's in love with every book in the store. He doesn't want to sell any of them. He comes over and asks what I'm looking for and then he tells me the history of it and the love story he has with each book and how he got it."

The thought of the boy, forced into *Brigadoon*, walking alone in the hot New Haven summer to the old bookstore, was too sad. The walk, the weather, the desire to look at old books in summer rather than play a sport outside or even go kayaking alone, the suspicions of the ponytailed old hippie owner—it added up to a picture of unbearable sadness.

"I told him I was looking for Alan Sherman's biography. He had no respect for the book and said it would be hard to find, and expensive."

"I think I can find it for you," I said.

"I'll pay any price," he said. "Up to a hundred dollars."

The book was located immediately at Powell's in Oregon. The price was five dollars. When I mailed it to him and his mother got him to call to say thank you, he started guessing the price, and as I had to say lower with each guess, he became more interested. He liked a bargain as well as the idea of having big bucks. When he was sixteen he'd spent the day in Venice on a school trip to Slovenia and bought a counterfeit Rolex watch for five dollars by walking away from the vendor's best offer. He'd always taken pride in the transaction.

I FELL into an anxious acceptance of not knowing about the boy's life.

The summer of the yoga ball, one of the last normal summers for the world, he told me that he was going to a woman psychiatrist. He said he called her by her first name. "She's Persian," he said, telling me her name as a punch line. He loved to say foreign names, and had kept his childhood amusement at hearing anything that wasn't American. He said he believed the psychiatrist had started to dress better because of his influence. First she wore plain suits; after a few visits, she began to wear silk shirts and slacks, or dresses.

"I think she's changed her style for me," he said seriously. I knew that with psychotherapists anything was possible, but it sounded ridiculous. I myself had gotten a psychiatrist to switch from black oxfords to sneakers. "Only nuns and priests wear black shoes in summer," I had told him. Fear of association with that group must have propelled him into action.

The night of the all-night call was the time we discussed his psychiatrist's wardrobe—one of our many topics. Later, when I looked back I tried to figure out which drug he had been using. When he described his doctor, he sounded as if the whole thing was another adventure in which he was the audience for the antics of the human race.

He said he had decided to stop seeing friends who used him as their entertainment. He'd realized that most people said their dull ordinary sentences and waited for him to speak so they could laugh.

I told the boy that I knew what he meant and I had given up socializing with the dull, and then had to give up socializing altogether. I gave a few examples of the things people spoke about, how they all said the same thing. "Usually a thing they've read in a magazine or heard someone else say on television," he said before I could say it.

"The majority of people have no original thoughts," the boy said.

. . .

WHERE WE lived in the winter, some alumnae of various junior colleges had formed a "book club." The two ringleaders of the club had even graduated from real colleges, so the job fell to them to lead the club. From what they said when I met any of them on the street, the book was always the one that everyone in America had heard of that day. One word the junior-college graduates had learned in the book club was "accessible." I always changed the subject.

The boy understood when I described the women in the book club. He knew their type, he said, and their nail polish, from his parents' circle of the bourgeoisie, as he liked to call them.

When he was eleven or twelve, he used to describe their situations in the suburbs of Boston. He told the story of one woman: "Her marriage is unraveling." Her husband had an apartment in London and a mistress. He'd given up his science professorship at the university to pursue a career in art. His art was making mandolins out of tinfoil. Their cat had drunk some antifreeze and almost died, or did die. The boy couldn't be sure.

"How do you know that?" I'd asked him.

"Well, she comes over to have coffee with my mother and they're in the kitchen talking and I go in on the pretext of boiling water for tea."

I asked what the woman would do if they split up. "She has her cat—I think she has the cat, it might be dead—and her garden . . . and her job as a part-time cake baker," he said.

THAT NIGHT of the yoga-ball call he'd mentioned that he had started to go to psychotherapy in high school and he said that he liked the doctor because he wore Turnbull & Asser shirts. I saw that he was on the path of liking psychotherapists for the wrong reasons, but I didn't get into the subject. He was a novice. He'd learn.

"Oh, the shirts," I said. I told him that I had seen a psychiatrist for a year because of his shirts.

"What kind were they?" the boy asked.

"Tattered old Brooks Brothers. And he had corduroy slacks that had no corduroy lines left. The legs looked like cardboard."

"That can be an affectation, too," the boy said.

"Yes, but I figured it out too late," I said. "I'd seen ones wearing so many worse shirts—big stripes with starched white collars and cuffs, for example—I was desperate."

"I can understand that," he said.

THE BOURGEOIS BLUES

Dᴜʀɪɴɢ ᴛʜᴇ ᴅᴀʀᴋ winter months of not knowing what his life was in California, I assumed that neither the boy nor his parents wished to speak to me because of something bad about myself. The something could be any number of notions they'd gotten me to worry about, from not blow-drying my hair to not knowing which restaurants Robert De Niro owned in New York.

When his mother first asked about one of these restaurants in 1991 and I said, "I don't know anything about it," his father shouted, "She doesn't know about Robert De Niro's restaurants! She lives as a recluse in the country!"

I had never thought of the word "recluse" this way. I thought I was seeking peace, like Thoreau, or even not like him. I had a lifelong feeling of inferiority to Thoreau, and later on to Christiane Amanpour, Martha Stewart, Emily Dickinson, Elvis Presley, Georgia O'Keeffe, Rachel Carson, Eudora Welty, and Greta Van Susteren before she changed networks.

AT FIRST when he started college, the boy said he loved New York compared with Boston. After a few weeks, he changed his mind and said, "They're all from New Jersey. They come in limos to go to restaurants on Park Avenue South." He also hated downtown, especially Greenwich Village, where he went to college. "Everyone looks like Salman Rushdie," he said. He wished he could live on the Upper East Side, on Fifth Avenue.

I told him it was noisy from the roar of the buses, and that the air was dirty from the fumes.

"Then Park Avenue would be okay," he said.

DAYS OF LATE SPRING

T HE CREEPY YEAR continued on this way. Until one day, in the spring, the boy called. He was all excited, or all up. After the Creative Monsters call he'd never wanted to talk.

I was happy to hear from him. And even worse, I assumed his good mood meant that he was getting better.

"You'll never believe this," he said. "I'm walking outside, it's actually a beautiful day, but you have to promise not to tell anyone." It was this: a famous professor somewhere on the other coast had been promoted to chairman even though he had a low IQ.

He continued talking in an overexcited voice as he described the political system in academia. I wondered why this subject was of sufficient interest to require a call from his cell phone out in the street in the middle of the day. I didn't even know they had streets in Beverly Hills.

All I knew was what I'd seen on TV news about the trial of an infamous murderer. The killer's house and garden were shown, and outside the front entrance there was a big beautiful lavender flower, an agapanthus. That's how I knew that landscape gardeners could be hired by anyone to design flower gardens, but I never saw a sidewalk.

"By the way, don't you think there's something wrong with my parents, the way they were willing to pack up and move back and forth across the country and do over another house every few years?"

I thought about it for a second. While I was still thinking, he said, "Shouldn't they want to make lasting friends and associates and be connected to a place?"

"They have a lot of friends," I said. When I thought about them and their friends, it reminded me of high school. Back then, they were trying to do all the things the normal kids did, maybe even appear on *American Bandstand.* They'd talked about this with me.

"They have no real friends," the boy said.

"I thought they did," I said.

"Have you noticed that my father doesn't know how to talk to anyone? He can't have a conversation."

"But he says things that are so funny, everyone wants to be around him."

"That's not talking," the boy said. "He doesn't know how to relate to other human beings in real conversation. Haven't you noticed this?"

"I thought that was just with me," I said.

"No, that's with everyone," the boy said. "But someday he'll have to face it, and he won't."

"Maybe he can get away without facing it," I said. "He's gotten this far and he's been successful."

"It's an empty success," the boy said. "And he's trying to deny that. But I'm almost home. I'll call you when I get inside the house, in five minutes."

"Will you really?" I said. "Because I have to go out to photograph a pond before the light is gone."

"I will. Five minutes, I swear," he said.

Half an hour passed as I got ready to go out. I called him on his cell phone and there was no answer. I called on the regular phone and the machine answered. Then I left. I called him that night. Maybe five days passed before he answered. I wondered what he was doing during this time.

"Oh, right. I was supposed to call you," he said. "But my mother was there and I had to placate her about a number of things."

I didn't ask about the things. Maybe he'd been out on a dope-buying expedition and she was questioning him about his activities.

He was glad to get right back to talking about everyone's psychological makeup.

"Those who suffer from lack of self-esteem will never recover. Everything in life is a fraud. Most married people should never have gotten married. Most couples' relationships are based on mutual low self-esteem and pity."

"You mean empathy—not pity," I said. But first the choice of the word "pity" made me laugh and the laughter spread out and into my chest, right where all the anxiety was stored, and took its place.

"It's the same thing," he said in his cold way.

"What about love?" I found myself saying, even though it sounded like a bad song title.

"People delude themselves about that. Usually it's just a need for them to think they're better than they know they are."

"You mean you don't believe in love?" I said. It was the bad song again. Songs with lyrics like these had forced me to leave stores. The one with "the thing called love" had driven me out of many places. I was saving up for the three-hundred-dollar price of the Bose silencing headphones and in the meantime often left the discount drugstore without looking through all the Reach toothbrushes.

"You know about this. *You're* an existentialist," he said.

"I am?" I said. I was surprised to hear it. For a minute I couldn't even remember what existentialism was—as applied to myself, anyway. I'd been trying to forget about it since I was his age.

The play *No Exit* was performed on television, in my late childhood, while my mother was lying on the couch after a hard day of teaching grammar to juvenile delinquents. She was watching the play on the Motorola wood-cabinet television but told me to leave the room at the part where Colleen Dewhurst was stuffing the towels under the door to keep the gas from escaping and foiling the suicide plans.

"What are they doing with the towels?" I asked.

"Don't watch," she'd said. "Go do your homework. Practice your piano lessons."

"Why are you watching?" I asked.

"It's not for children," she said. "There's rarely any serious drama on television. I want to see it." She disapproved of my choices, *Ozzie and Harriet* and *I Love Lucy*.

That was my first brush with existentialism. "I got over it after college," I told the boy.

"But you're a Nietzschean," he said.

For a second I was flattered. It sounded good. I quickly tried to remember the writings of Nietzsche, but could think only of *Nietzsche's Last Days*, a review of a biography—and the part with the mad philosopher talking to a horse at the end of his sad life.

"I decided not to dwell on it," I said.

"How come? You know he's right," he said threateningly.

"A boyfriend I had at the time talked me out of it. Then there were the Beatles. My next boyfriend dedicated himself to music and distracted himself with the album *Rubber Soul*."

"The Beatles?" the boy said. "It makes no sense."

"This boyfriend said, 'Which is more fun, Nietzsche or the Beatles?' He was always looking for ways to have fun."

"Rather simpleminded," the boy said.

"But he was right. Also involved was the element of romance." I decided not to say the word "sex" to the boy. He could put two and two together for himself. And also because he'd told me that his parents had confronted him with questions about his relationships with girls.

"Isn't that a personal matter?" I'd said.

"I think my parents are afraid that I turned to drugs to escape the knowledge of being gay. Can you believe that?"

"I can't believe confronting someone with such a question," I said. "Or that they would even think it. You must have misunderstood."

"No. And I'm furious that the next psychiatrist had the same idea! The psychiatrist is, like, 'Can't you see how people might think that you are?' "

"What!" I said. "Why?"

"Because of the way I dress."

"How? Khaki pants and button-down shirts? Oh, and the sport jackets?"

"Yes! Can you believe that? Because my shirts are neatly pressed, and the way I sit."

"How? A ballet position?" I said.

The boy laughed. Or more scoffed and laughed at the same time. "You'd think it was, from the way they act. With crossed legs, I said, 'European men dress and sit this way.' "

"Is this what psychiatrists do now?"

"I'm being hounded on all sides! I have to run away to New York. There's no choice left to me."

"You could wait it out. Try to find some better doctors," I'd said.

Suddenly he started quoting Nietzsche at length. Though I was a fan, I couldn't get into it. I couldn't stand it. I thought of adding Schopenhauer, or Spinoza, for a real break—I'd read in the introduction to his work that Spinoza had had a disagreement with his sister about a piece of inherited furniture—but still, adding the two philosophers might make it worse. Now this new twist to the situation. The boy's problems were mounting in an unbearable way.

"Everyone thinks about these things in college," I said. "But then you figure, you're alive, make the best of it. Or something."

"Like how? There's no point to anything," he said.

"Work, love, nature, books, poems, music, traveling, trees, birds, butterflies, flowers." It sounded like something said by a follower of Norman Vincent Peale. And a Viennese psychoanalyst had told me that Freud hated music.

I wanted to read him a quote from *British Butterflies,* an antique butterfly book: "We live ... for moments ... minutes— fractions of an hour ... for these intervals are timeless. While they last, we have complete understanding, happiness and strength. We live in the true sense and we perceive the meaning of life. This experience is mine while I watch butterflies. I love these mysterious beings and as I dwell in the country ... in a place favoured by butterflies, my perfect moments are many...." I wanted to read this to a heroin addict.

"Everyone tells me that," he said before I tried out the quote. "I don't see the point to anything," he said.

"Work and love—Freud said that."

"Freud was an opium addict," the boy said.

"Only after he was at an advanced age in his life," I said. "And it was for pain from an illness."

"True. But all kids my age don't think about this. They're idiots. Some kids I know go right out into the world of jobs and society without thinking about anything."

I thought that as a joke I might quote the first line of the most famous poem by Joyce Kilmer.

"Don't you have trees in California?" I said.

"Of course! It's Beverly Hills. We have palm trees, too."

"Maybe you're worn out from the rehab and the withdrawal and the life disruption."

He skipped right over that and said, "I'd like to travel. I'd like to just travel for my whole life!"

"You could. You could get a job reporting on everything. Remember your trip to Slovenia in high school? You reported to everyone on that."

He had been dragged on that school trip the way he'd been

forced into *Brigadoon.* "Who set the itinerary to Slovenia?" I'd asked when he announced the news in his morose way.

"The teacher," he said.

"I bet he has Sloveniak relatives he wants to see and the trip is a front for that," I said.

"It's true, he does have relatives there. We're going to Venice and Greece, too. But you're right, the most time is in Slovenia."

When he returned, he said, "The whole trip was comprised of sitting on buses, waiting."

He said he'd been given horrible dumplings and puddings to eat in the homes of the Slovenians.

"They watch you every second, every bite, to make sure you're eating the dumplings and puddings. One day I couldn't stand it anymore and I left. I walked to the nearest hotel."

"How far away was it?"

"About four hours. I'm on these dusty roads with donkeys and mules, I'm carrying my suitcases and raincoat in the blazing sun. I'm breathing sand and dirt and passing by bandits and beggars the whole way. I have no water. I get to the hotel and they don't think I have money for a room, I'm just a kid. So I give them my American Express card and finally they take me to a room they've hastily cleaned out from the last guest, who departed one second before.

"There's an ashtray with a cigarette butt still going in it and someone's jacket on the chair. Maybe it's the owner's room, who knows. I opened the window and went to sleep for a few hours."

"You were brave to do all that," I said. I was impressed. "Did you get a bottle of water?"

"Yes—an inferior brand. I called my parents to inform them,

and they're, like, 'Okay, go meet the tour back at the hotel and fly home with them.'

"The teachers were, like, 'We'll report you for this behavior,' and I'm, like, 'Fine. My parents didn't know we'd be in Slovenia for ten days when they sent me on this expensive trip.' "

"Why don't you report them to the principal? Do they still have principals?" I pictured a free-for-all school system and society, the signs of which I saw everywhere.

"Sort of. Not the way you think from your high school. We talked about it. We all said we'd do it when we got back. But then you get back, you have to unpack, you get back into your life, gradually you forget about it."

"If it happened to me, I'd be composing letters and making phone calls for weeks afterwards," I said.

"What's the point? It's more time wasted."

"I keep telling you I've wasted my life. Now you see how," I said.

"Not really," he said. "That's not an example."

DRUGS PRESCRIBED
BY AN ADDICT

IN THE SPRING, during that last year of his attempted drug rehabilitation, the boy had begun prescribing medication whenever we spoke on the phone. I told him I took double the maximum dose of Saint-John's-wort during the day and valerian at night to sleep.

"Does it work?" he asked.

"No," I said. "In the beginning, yes, but then the life situation continued on and the botanical remedies couldn't keep up with the pace. I was given samples of real drugs."

"Like what? What did you take?" he asked with too much sudden interest.

"Nothing. I took the samples home but couldn't get myself to take the pills."

"Like which ones?" he asked.

I rattled off all the names like a professional user of medications. "I stared at them. I read the tiny print of the pamphlets inside. One had two-tone pink granules in a gelatin capsule and a thirty-seven-percent rate of bad side effects." Another one was turquoise blue with a smile-face printed with letters of the drug's name. When I saw that, I threw out the whole batch.

Sometime later I came across the *New York Times* obituary of the man who invented the smile face. I had never known such a thing had to be invented by an actual person. It seemed more like the work of an idiot or some of the other feebleminded— work done in their spare time while waiting for psychiatric help in an institution. Still, I could feel only sympathy for the man, and sorry about his demise.

"I know a kid who took that pink one. It changed his life," the boy said.

"Kids are different," I said, thinking about those with decades of time ahead of them to get straightened out.

"I've taken it with no effects—good or bad," he said.

Then we got on to the anti-anxieties.

"Xanax and the benzodiazepines are addictive," he said with authority.

"I forget all about taking one unless a panic comes on," I said.

"How often is that?" he asked.

"Not that often. Just when I think about the future and the past and the present," I said. This was still before the new world situation.

"They produce euphoria, which causes the addiction," he said.

"I never felt any euphoria. If you take it for anxiety, you just get back to normal."

"Kids take it to produce euphoria," he insisted.

"Why can't they get euphoria from life?" I said as a cliché, but didn't wait for the answer. "Have you tried Xanax?" I asked.

"They won't give the drug patients benzodiazepines. They gave me Clonidine for a while. You should try it."

WHICHEVER DRUG he suggested, the busy doctor I consulted— distracted by his many psychotic patients—was glad to prescribe. But the doctor took a guess that the drug recommended by my friend was Klonopin.

I reported to the boy, "Too drugged and dopey."

"*Clonidine,* not Klonopin! You got the wrong one," he said. "You didn't like that feeling?"

"You can't do anything in that condition." I pictured some opium dens I'd seen in photographs and movies. "What's the point?" I said.

"You didn't like it?" he asked with interest.

"For surgery, not for daily life," I said.

"You should try Neurontin," he said. "That's what I have now."

"What for?"

"Hypomania, supposedly. It's an anti-seizure drug, now thrown in with everything to combat anxiety."

Even with that recommendation, I asked the psychiatrist for some. As he gladly wrote it out, I noticed his wastebasket filled with carbon papers from triplicate prescription forms. I had a feeling of revulsion at joining in with the basket of forms.

I WAS thinking about the first time the name of a pill had come up in discussion between us. In early childhood, the boy had been stung by a poisonous jellyfish. He had told me this story when he was twelve. He'd been on vacation with his family. "My recollection is that I was six or seven," he said. "When I came out of the water, my entire body was covered with stinging, red welts. My parents did nothing."

"What about your father, being a doctor and all that?"

"He was the most callous one. 'It'll go away by itself,' he said. Can you believe that?"

"Didn't they give you some Benadryl?"

"Nothing. They all walked away talking to each other as if nothing had happened. I was left to tag along behind them. I was crying! They didn't even notice."

I asked if they gave him some treatment when they got home.

"Nothing! They put me to bed, where I lay suffering. Maybe they gave me a Benadryl then and left me while they chatted on. Finally I sank into a painful sleep."

"It doesn't sound like your parents," I said.

"A father who's a doctor means nothing in a case like this. It's not his specialty. He says it's nothing, whatever it is."

"Would he remove a splinter?"

"He's performed minor surgery on the kitchen table. I've learned not to show him anything. He uses no local anesthesia and keeps saying, 'It doesn't hurt.' If I have anything requiring first aid, I tell my mother in secret so we can go to a regular doctor the next day."

THE SHORT PHONE
CALLS OF JUNE

The last weeks of spring coincided with a series of surprise daytime phone calls from my friend the boy. Sometimes I tried to postpone the calls until later, when I'd have more time to talk to him about his two subjects: existentialism and the meaninglessness of life. Other times I spent an hour talking whenever he wanted to.

"Later is hard," he said. "It's when I have to be with my father."

When I asked his father whether he'd rather I didn't talk to the boy, he said, "He needs to talk to people his own age."

"He talks to your oddball friends as practice for his real life."

"How is it practice?" he asked.

"It gives him confidence," I said.

"Why doesn't he have friends his own age?"

"I thought he did. I heard him talking to various kids in the background when he was in New York in college."

"Which year of college?"

"First year. Then I never heard from him again until last summer."

"Why did you think that was?"

"I wondered why. Then I figured he didn't need us anymore. I thought maybe it was a healthy sign." Whenever I'd seen him before, the only times he'd acted happy or showed affection was with his dog. In this way he was like David Letterman.

I remembered the last time I saw the boy, during his first year of college. It was at a dinner to celebrate the publication of a book of my photographs. About a week after the dinner, he and I reviewed the event.

Since the one thing he'd respected most that I'd ever done— and maybe the only thing—was my purchase on sale of that pale peach Armani linen jacket, I asked him if he'd noticed the white linen Armani shirt worn for the dinner. It was fifteen years old and had been found for half price at the old Barneys on Seventeenth Street.

"The shoulders seemed puffy," he said.

"You mean the shoulder pads?" I said. "They were small ones."

"Something had a puffed-up look," he said.

"I took them out and hastily sewed them in at a better angle, but they still looked too high," I explained with regret at the thought of the whole situation. A person at my station of life should have a seamstress for small sewing jobs. But in the small crazy town where we lived, the one seamstress lost whatever people gave her and took four months to obtain snaps.

"Were you crying when the champagne came?" he asked.

"Crying? Of course not. Why would you think that?" I said.

"I thought I saw some trembling in the shoulder area," he said.

"Those must have been the shoulder pads bobbing around. I didn't have time to sew them in right. Unless I was trembling with fear that people would be drinking more."

"I thought maybe you were crying."

"It wasn't the Academy Awards," I said. "You were in L.A. too long."

"I was there for the one summer. You think it could happen so fast?"

"If you're into the crying thing," I said. "Remember Sammy Maudlin on *SCTV*?"

"Yes, yes," he said, almost laughing. I realized that I'd never heard him really laugh. He loved John Candy the most and once said with grief, "How can John Candy be dead?"

I knew exactly what he meant, so I said, "I know what you mean."

"By the way, everyone was drunk at the dinner. Did you notice?" he said.

"Except for you and me. I drank Pellegrino, you drank Coke. By the way, aren't you too old to order Coke at the best Japanese restaurant?"

"No, but I meant the alcohol—your cousin had eight sakes."

"You were counting?" I said.

"Yes. And his wife had almost as many," the boy said accusingly.

"How about my husband?" I asked.

"He had a lot. Wine, beer, sake, everything."

"I told you about this. Now you see my predicament firsthand," I said.

"Everyone's drunk. You have to face it—you don't like alcohol, you have no choice. . . . You could socialize with non-
drinkers only."

"Yes, but I can't find any. Except from AA."

"They're in their own partition of the world," he said. "You
couldn't join anyway."

I had noticed something at the dinner: The boy's father fell
in love with my cousin's wife; my close friend, an intoxicated
landscape designer, fell in love with the boy's father even though
he was acting and looking like Rick Moranis as a Hollywood pro-
ducer on *SCTV;* the art director fell in love with the landscape designer even though, or because, she wore no makeup; my cousin's
wife continued to love her own husband; he in turn loved whatever he was saying; my husband was in love with the wine. With
all this going on, I couldn't feel love for anything, not even the
publication of my photographs, because I knew those shoulder
pads weren't quite right, and the vestiges of my past narcissism
had been whittled down to a place where I had no self.

Love was all around in all the wrong places—a typical dinner
downtown in New York City a few years before the new world
circumstances.

The room was overheated and the diners were dressed in
black—like the bellhop in *Heartbreak Hotel*—and they were
talking in loud voices. And there was the degradation of the
knowledge of how the reservation had been made: calling one
month in advance, but not a month plus a day—that was too
early; a month minus a day—that was too late.

We'd chosen the restaurant for the shiitake and maitake
mushrooms and the no-smoking rule, but the tension, heat, and
noise probably canceled out the immune-boosting properties of
the delicious mushrooms.

Worst of all was the sight of the boy, who was stranded and more alone than anyone, because he had no delusions about love or himself. He could only watch, hunched down in his chair, excruciatingly socially uncomfortable, in a completely separate state from all other beings.

THE DAY after I mentioned the word "confidence" to his father, the boy called from outside, somewhere in Beverly Hills.

"Did you tell my father I had low self-esteem?" he said. I pictured him walking along saying this sentence into his phone.

"Certainly not." I told him what I'd said, summing it up as "I said it was good practice for you to talk to his friends. But never mind. I won't ever discuss you with him again."

"Good, because he misunderstands everything. I'll call you when I get home, in five minutes."

A week later he called again from the street or whatever they have in Beverly Hills.

"Did you tell my father I can't love?" he said again into his cell phone.

"Of course not. I said you were too cool to show any emotion. But forget it. I'll never tell him anything about you again."

"Good. Because he doesn't understand existentialism. He thinks he does. I'll call you back in five minutes."

THE FIVE minutes went on for a few days. When I reached him on his cell phone, he sounded tired. "Were you sleeping?" I asked.

"No. I was lying down on my bed and resting." He had a new, weary voice I'd never heard, heartbreakingly weary. Even if he was still an addict, I didn't care. It was just as heartbreaking.

"Should we hang up?" I asked.

"No. I'm just waiting for my mother to go look at some lawn furniture at Bloomingdale's."

"That's like what you used to do in junior high school," I said. Once he'd told me about an outing: "I went with my father to meet two rabbis at Legal Seafood." This was during the era in which everything he talked about made me laugh.

"I know, it's pathetic!" he said. "I have no life. When I think about my life in New York, it seems like a dream, and now I'm back to where I was before."

"It's not so bad to go and look at lawn furniture," I said. "People seek out your advice."

I couldn't help thinking at the same time that I didn't know there was a Bloomingdale's in Los Angeles, the way I hadn't known that everyone in Los Angeles originally came from Brooklyn or the Bronx. I thought people in California were really from California. I couldn't see even the store's name fitting into the city of Los Angeles. I had spent too much time in that store in New York searching for Armani shirts on sale before that block and neighborhood had become ruined in the 1980s. Something was wrong with me that I used to walk around Fifty-ninth Street and Lexington Avenue trying to find one Armani shirt.

The last time I'd searched for an Armani shirt, something happened that made it the final time. The Armani store had moved to a new, larger, and worse location.

Since I could go to Madison Avenue only after dark, in winter, I'd been there without having to see the new building in daylight. The sky was always dark and all the buildings disappeared, with only their windows lit and visible. But I hadn't been warned about the interior, a large meaningless space—several floors of spaces—with the clothing hidden away behind secret panels.

I was dressed inappropriately for the Armani store, in an old olive green gabardine man's-style coat and dark green walking boots. The worst part of my appearance was the worn-out tan canvas Danish book bag. It was overstuffed with books, papers, a camera, a glass bottle of Mountain Valley water, a small bag of daily cosmetics, and an apple. The carrying of this bag had caused permanent tendinitis in my shoulder, which could be helped only by acupuncture with a Chinese medical doctor I couldn't get to because his office was in an overheated building on the most crowded Midtown street in the East Forties. On the same shoulder I carried a smaller canvas bag for important things: a few dollars, a credit card, Xanax, Tylenol, Kleenex, pens, sunglasses, and a bottle of echinacea. Even so, I was treated with decency and respect by the woman salesperson.

On the way up the staircase to the shirt floor, I realized I was weak from not having eaten anything except for a small serving of steel-cut oats, several hours before. I took the apple out of the bag. I had cut the apple in half, and had wrapped it in a napkin and put it in a plastic bag. I thought I could take one bite unobtrusively in order to keep from fainting. But as I took the furtive bite of the apple while on the carpeted marble staircase, I immediately felt this was wrong—Jacqueline Kennedy wouldn't have done it—and I put the apple back in its plastic bag before I reached the landing.

The boy's mother had once asked me to meet her at the Forbes museum when she was in New York. She wanted to see the Fabergé egg collection and I agreed because the museum was downtown, near where we lived at the time. While wandering around the gallery hoping to find something to see other than the eggs, I came across a sliver of an upper-class society woman all in black. The woman was standing still as a statue, except for one hand, which she was using to furtively comb her hair. I could tell that she was desperate, or insane in some way.

When I was in the Armani dressing room waiting for a shirt to be brought to me from the secret closet of other styles and sizes, I didn't like looking at my reflection in the mirror—myself without a shirt on, my chest not as flat as in the past, a grown-up-looking bra reminiscent of the foundation garments my mother wore. I reached for my old beige cardigan sweater, the one I'd been wearing at the discount drugstore. I pulled it on without buttoning it and held it together with one hand while I took the apple out of the bag with the other hand.

The salesperson was taking a long time to find one white shirt and would probably appear with six or eight satin things—blue, gray, and tan. I was never prepared for this moment; after I said white or off-white, they always brought blue and gray. They must not know that color affects the mind. Then I saw myself in the mirror. I was holding the sweater closed with one arm and holding the apple in the other hand. The look was one I'd seen in photographs of European refugees on a roadside after the war, half clothed and eating a scrap of bread given by rescuing soldiers. At the same time, I saw a tinge of slight glamour in the mirror. It startled me, because I'd never wear a V-necked cardigan sweater without a shirt underneath, and it had the look of a pinup girl from 1948.

IN THE boy's case, I thought Los Angeles had its own kinds of stores, stores I'd heard mentioned in reruns of the George Burns and Gracie Allen show.

But I was worried about why he was resting. I pictured him recovering from a drug and gearing up to act like a normal boy.

"She'll be calling me any minute," he said. "I can't be caught on the phone."

"It's good for you to have friends. They know that."

"They're suspicious of all calls," he said with resignation.

"I thought that was in the past," I said.

"It is, but they'll never trust me again. She's coming upstairs. Yes? Mom? I'm here. I'm ready. It's on the kitchen table. Okay, I'll call you later," he said, and hung up.

THE POINT OF LIFE

T HE DAYTIME CALLS stopped for a while and then changed into sadder conversations when I called him. To distract him from his problems, I told him about a disagreement I was having with a publisher. He loved to solve problems of commerce and money.

"I realize *no one can be happy*!" he said with a deep new misery, "*All* people are *unhappy*."

"That's not true," I said. "It just seems that way because you talk to people my age. You have thirty more years of fun ahead," I said as a lie. I knew that things could boomerang back in the fifties.

"Like what fun?" he said.

"Like everything." I was thinking of a television biography I'd seen about Elvis Presley. A fan, now a grown-up woman who looked older than my age, said that Elvis "like everyone else does, got to be middle-aged, and at that age, worn down by the

burdens of the world, he brought a different talent to his perfor-
mances than the one he'd had as a young person." As the woman
said this, photos were shown of the overweight drug-puffed-up
Elvis with his sideburns and white satin jumpsuit, in the 1970s.

I didn't tell the boy what I was thinking about. I tried to
change the subject. First I said, "I thought it would be amusing
for you to hear about a financial dispute, but you have your own
serious situation."

"I do. They're insisting I go stay with my cousin in Philadelphia for the weekend. And it's my birthday on top of everything
else. I have nothing to say to him. He's the one who started this.
He told my parents about the drug suspicion. I regret coming
out here. I regret telling my parents and family anything! It's a
year of my life wasted." Then he said, in the saddest voice, "A
lost year."

"One year now will seem like a week when you look back on
it," I said with false knowledge.

"I used to think, How can I mine this experience for something?" he said. "But now I see it's hopeless."

"You can. Did you ever read *A Mother's Kisses?*" I asked one
more time. "He mined a terrible year of life into a great book."

"I read a little. But this is worse than that kid's situation."

"Why are you going to Philadelphia?" I asked.

"For *fun.* Can you believe that? We're supposed to have fun
together."

"It is the city of brotherly love," I said.

"Right," the boy agreed with a new kind of cynicism. Because he used to love his family and to like going places with
them. There was the time he went to a restaurant in New York
and he'd been given a pieful of leeks.

"What will I do in Philadelphia? Then we're going to the family beach house. What will I do there?"

"What did you do before? You had fun."

"That was a different time. And I'm expected to start graduate school soon!"

"How soon?" I imagined the mess and pressure of his life.

"August!" he said with dread of a new kind, though I knew it was a dreaded month for many reasons. "I can't do it! I'm trapped!" he said.

"You can go to another doctor in Philadelphia. Wasn't that the plan?"

"I have an appointment. But I have to see a second one for drugs."

"That's the way it goes," I said. "You can describe the doctors and their offices to everyone."

"I don't have *time* for all these *appointments*!" he said.

"Join the club," I said. I thought of my friends in this club. First the psychotherapy, then the couples' therapy, then the separate psychotherapy for the spouse. Then realizing there was too much of this, too many appointments and too much expense and time—to say nothing of the crew of unprofessionals. Then came giving it all up and having to be whatever you were.

THE BIRTHDAY WEEKEND

OVER THE WEEKEND I forgot about the Philadelphia plan. He'd said his parents were going away to a medical conference in Nantucket.

"Why don't you go with them?" I'd said. "June is the best month, along with September."

"I wasn't invited," he said. "It's all meetings and conferences."

I remembered the drug scene I'd read about on the front page of the Nantucket newspaper. It seemed as if people died of heroin overdoses every week. Or there were arrests and drug busts involving a big cache of heroin. I could see him slinking around at night buying some.

On Saturday night I called him on his cell phone.

"This is weird," he said. "I was lying on the bed and the phone was in my jacket pocket, in the closet. I thought it was vibrating, I looked at it, I heard it ring, and it was you."

"Where are you?" I said.

"In Philadelphia. In my cousin's apartment. It's a nightmare. I'm their prisoner."

"Why are you in bed?" I asked.

"I'm tired. The hellish nightmare of coast-to-coast plane travel wears me out."

"What's the plan for the evening?" I asked.

"Oh, they brought in a horrible dinner I couldn't eat. I said, 'Let's go get *ice cream*!' So we did that," he said with strange satisfaction. "But then I wanted some Coke to drink and my cousin said, 'No more caffeine today.' I'm treated like a child."

But first there was the candy insult. He said his parents had been suspicious when he asked his mother to get more of the green-tea candy she'd bought him. It occurred to me that it was the only form of green tea she'd ever bought. The whole family drank diet soda and ate food of the style of the 1950s.

"She's bought me candy my *whole life*!" he said. He named the candy, all kinds of candy I'd seen around at drugstores during my lifetime. "And *now* she's suspicious.

"Then after the ice cream I bought some chocolate-covered apricots," he said.

"Chocolate-covered—dried?" I said.

"Yes, do you know them?"

"Yes."

"Do you like them?"

"Not 'in conjunction with each other,' as you would have said when you were eleven."

He laughed a weak laugh. "What would I say now?" he asked, as if he were trying to think back kindly of himself as a child.

"Something more elaborate and exact," I said.

"But why is it suspicious—the candy?" he asked.

"Well—the ice cream, the Coke drinking, the candies, and now the chocolate apricots. No food, all sweets. It adds up," I said.

"There's nothing to eat here! I'm hungry!" he said in a new, belligerent style, as if he'd been cornered by the evidence.

"You can go out and buy something," I said.

"It's not New York. Everything is closed."

"You're a grown-up. You lived on your own," I said, still trying to believe the story.

"I know, I'm an idiot!" he said. "I can't do anything anymore."

"You're just in difficult circumstances," I said. "They must have some fruit. And bread." I still believed him, and that he might be hungry.

"I ate some peanuts I found in the cabinet. Now I'm thirsty."

"Drink some bottled water," I said.

"I want a Coke!" he said, sounding like a child. "If they hear me go out, they'll suspect something."

"Ask them to go with you," I said.

He tried to laugh. It was more like a smirk I could hear. "I can't give him the satisfaction . . . Okay, I'm looking in the kitchen, I see they have bananas."

"You could eat a banana. And toast," I said.

"Okay, good idea," he said. "They have bread. Marble rye."

"Marble rye!" I said.

"What's funny?" he said.

"It's the worst bread, a joke bread, always left over in all-night delis. It's dyed with caramel color to get the dark part." I'd seen this bread when I'd had to go to these kinds of delis to buy chocolate late at night when I was in college.

"I'll make some toast," he said, as if he'd solved a difficult problem.

"Then you'll have what Elvis ate—peanuts, bananas, and bread—his sandwich."

"But he *fried* it! I'm not starting crashing pans around now!" he said in his funniest way. "They're asleep in the next room."

After his dinner of bread and bananas he would call back, he said. "Or you call me on my cell phone. I can't talk in the kitchen or I might wake them."

I WAS thinking that underneath this conversation of mixed phone babysitting and friendship he meant he needed his drugs and couldn't figure out how to get them in a city where he was unfamiliar with the drug scene. Or he had some with him and couldn't use them in such close quarters with his cousin and cousin's wife. A young couple, working diligently in promising careers—one involving *Beowulf*—and they had this situation in the guest room, I was thinking at the same time.

He had described the apartment to me: In order to open the door to his bathroom he had to sit on the bed, there was so little room for a person in the room—a former maid's room. There were no windows to be seen or looked through unless he put his head at the foot of the bed and twisted himself around.

When I called him back, he seemed to have calmed down. But he said he hadn't eaten the toast or the banana. He said he'd fallen asleep. He could hear his cousin talking in the other room. The close quarters infuriated him. He had planned to live in a large mansion by the age of twenty-five. Now he was living like a twenty-one-year-old junkie, eating peanuts in a tiny room.

"I'm trying to find something on television," he said in a voice of resentment of his state. We had the same channel on, without any sound, and a piece of phony-looking black-and-white film was on as part of something else.

"I'm in the mood to see an old black-and-white movie," he said, still in the belligerent voice.

"What's that on now?" I asked.

"I can't tell, but it's what put me in the mood," he said.

"Let's see what's on AMC," I said. There was no point expecting anything good when it was usually that colorized one with Rock Hudson as a doctor and Jane Wyman in the blind-patient romance part.

But there was my favorite movie, next to *The Stranger*— *Shadow of a Doubt.*

"We're lucky," I said to the boy. "But it's half over."

I saw Teresa Wright walking down the most pleasant American street, in Santa Rosa, 1941, on the way home from church. She was wearing white gloves and a hat with a gingham-and-white dress with a gingham Peter Pan collar. Whenever I watched the movie, I wished I owned the dress. In early childhood, in the fifties, I did own hand-me-down dresses similar to one the younger sister wore in the movie.

I wished I knew the families who lived in those houses in that town with sidewalks and trees and libraries and policemen on the corners. I was a sucker for all those things. When I first saw Thornton Wilder's name in the credits for the screenplay I understood why. His contribution must have given the movie the pure and unrealistic feeling of small-town life I knew to be an unattainable fantasy.

"I can't go on baking cakes," says Teresa Wright's mother, Emma Newton, in the movie when a photographer wants a photo of her mixing ingredients. She's already finished that stage of the cake, but he wants photos of normal American families doing their normal American things.

"Who's the man with that hat men wore?" he asked.

All the years I'd known him, he'd been fascinated by the 1950s and the brown felt hats that men wore in that decade and the two decades before. He'd seen the hats in movies and I'd seen the real hats during my childhood. But now he seemed too tired and weak to get into the subject. He asked no questions about the hat-wearing era he wished he'd lived in. This time he volunteered no stories about his relatives' hats, which hats he'd been offered, and which men he'd seen still wearing this kind of hat. "Rabbis," he once said. "They're the only ones who still wear them."

"That's the detective sent to investigate Teresa Wright's favorite uncle, Joseph Cotten," I said.

"What did he do, what crime?" he asked.

"They think he murdered wealthy widows for their inheritances."

"Did he do it?" he asked.

"You should watch the whole thing," I said. "I watch it at least once a year."

"The way some people watch *It's a Wonderful Life*," he said.

"Better, because it has the reality of evil. The other is too perfect."

"But you like that," he said, trying to get the energy to converse the way he used to.

"I like the beginnings of the Alfred Hitchcocks—the wholesome American family in the small town—before the bad thing happens. And also *The Stranger*. I love the part where Loretta

Young is hanging up the white organdy curtains when the Nazi war criminal knocks at the door."

"I can see why you'd like that," he said, sounding weaker.

"Should we watch it?" I said. "Or do you want to watch by yourself?"

"I'll do that," he said.

"Call me when it's over and give a review," I said.

"I will," he said. "Why are they in the garage?" he asked wearily.

"They're in love. He has to tell her the truth about her uncle, Joseph Cotten."

"Okay, I'll call you after," he said, and hung up.

When I didn't hear from him, I tried to believe he'd fallen asleep right after the movie ended.

I WATCHED the movie while the memory of the boy's situation was still pressing into my brain.

The characters in the movie had ideas similar to his. That was a part of the story I'd forgotten. Teresa Wright, about his age in a beginning scene, in a bad mood and appearing to be suffering from PMS—fortunately unnamed and undiagnosed at that time—is complaining, "People don't have real conversations. They just talk."

But before that scene, down in the big living room, the precocious younger sister says, "When I have a home of my own it's going to be full of well-sharpened pencils." That sounded like him, too, when he showed me around his well-organized room with tidy desk and supplies. Since the computer era had already begun, that many pencils were no longer necessary, but he did have quite a few, in addition to several pens in a special pen-holding jar. He supplied his parents' desks with pens, pencils, and paper for notes and messages, and he'd even organized this setup on the kitchen counter.

But soon Joseph Cotten enters and spoils the sunny picture by complaining about the state of the world. It's only supposed to be 1941 in the movie, but he's complaining that it's not the better world of his childhood.

After he shows his sister an old photograph of their parents, Teresa Wright looks at it and says: "How pretty she was."

"Everybody was sweet and pretty then," he replies in a scary way. "The whole world, it was a wonderful world, not like the world today, not like the world now. It was great to be young then. . . ."

Next he's lying down on the bed in the room of the beautiful old American house in the beautiful old small town—they've got those white organdy curtains, they have the flower-covered wallpaper, the wide hallways, the space for everything in every room—and he's looking back, he's ruminating in the style of the boy. I did this for years, too, until my exercise teacher told me, "Get up. Do something. Do anything."

Teresa Wright's mother is talking about Joseph Cotten—her brother, Teresa's uncle—what he was like when he was a boy. "He was such a quiet boy, always reading." After a bicycle accident in childhood where he fractured his skull, he was in a coma. "They wondered if he'd ever be the same," she explains.

By the middle of the movie, he's sounding just like my friend, the boy. "The world's a foul sty, the world's a hell. If you ripped the fronts off houses, you'd find swine . . ."

How could the boy have missed this movie? Especially because Joseph Cotten had just come from Philadelphia, where he'd been lying in bed in a rooming house, ruminating there, and smoking a cigar.

THE NEXT afternoon I called him. It was still his birthday weekend. He answered in a way described as "high as a kite." His voice scared me.

"How *ARE* you?" he called into the cell phone in a wild way, as if we hadn't spoken in ten years.

"Where are you?" I said.

"I'm at the Jersey shore, on the boardwalk. It's a beautiful day! I'm walking near the water, the air is fresh, the sun is out."

Since he'd never talked about the weather or the day with any enthusiasm, I understood it to mean he'd gotten some drug.

"What happened last night? I was awaiting your review," I said.

"I fell asleep. I didn't see the end," he said.

"Did you take your Neurontin today?" I asked.

"Not yet. Why?"

"You sound manic," I said.

"You're the *first person* I've spoken to *all day*! That's the reason. I'm *starved* for *conversation.*"

"Maybe you should take the Neurontin," I said.

"It's back at the house. I'll call you when I get there," he said, and hung up.

I CALLED him a few hours later. He still had the speedy tone in his voice.

"Have you taken your medicine yet?" I asked.

"It's downstairs," he said.

"Maybe you should go get it," I said.

"I will when we hang up."

During the weekend, I tried to talk to him and finish any of the conversations we'd started. Whenever he answered the phone at the house, he said he was upstairs and that he'd go to the phone downstairs, or he was downstairs and would go upstairs. I took this to be true, because we had agreed how much we hated being on stationary phones, trapped in one spot, unable to do many things at the same time.

But whenever he got to either phone, something interrupted. He said he'd call back.

Once he had a free minute and asked with camaraderie: "Have you taken your first Neurontin yet?"

"No, I'm waiting until Monday in case there's a side effect and I have to call a doctor."

"There are no side effects," he said. "I'm taking mine now."

"It's a big pill," I said.

"It's easy to take," he said with encouragement. "It goes down easily." I heard him swallow something. "It's coated. You should take it."

"Now I'm taking gigantic calcium tablets that I've choked on several times."

"You should break them in half," he said like an aficionado.

"Then when you swallow it, the broken part cuts your throat," I said.

"I've never encountered a problem with big pills," he said.

That was all we talked about. I still didn't know that recovering addicts love to talk drug talk.

THE BIRTHDAY

T HE DAY OF his birthday, I never reached him.

I left a message on his cell phone. As I said the sentence, I felt that I was a fool and my message was like one of a foolish, naïve aunt.

"You don't dress or look like an aunt," he'd said when we'd walked around Beacon Hill and I'd first expressed this aunt fear. "You won't be suspected of that," he added.

"I hope you're okay and that you had a happy birthday" was what I said into the phone for him to play back when he turned it on, even though I knew that both these wishes were impossible to come true.

When I didn't hear from him I imagined him listening to his cell phone answering-machine feature. I could see my sentence mixed in with messages from drug dealers. Maybe he'd get a laugh of irony when he heard it.

·   ·   ·

WHEN HE answered the phone, the weekend was over. He sounded fine. "Where are you?" I asked.

"Back in L.A. Why?" he said casually.

"I didn't hear from you. I was worried." I tried to sound equally casual.

"What do you mean 'worried'?" he asked with suspicion.

"Well, two days went by," I said.

"Oh well, we went to Philadelphia."

"What did you do on your birthday?" I asked.

"That was my birthday. Going to Philadelphia and walking around with my cousin."

I pictured them walking the hot, sunny, narrow city streets on a day in June. Anytime I saw people on the TV news in a city, especially in warm weather, I felt really sorry for them. I remembered myself in New York City in the hot, humid past.

The boy said he'd call back when he had more time. When that happened, he was all up again.

"We walked around the old part of Philadelphia," he said. "We saw the oldest street in America. It's all brick, with all these old brick houses. *Elspeth Alley.* You would have loved it!"

"Is it like Washington Mews?"

"Older, brickier, and more of it."

"Like Louisburg Square?" I said. I'd told him about that square when he was still in high school, and tried to get him to walk over there when we were in Boston one night. But he said he was too cold, dressed in a gray Chesterfield coat as if on the way to a private club from the 1950s.

"No, smaller-scale and less rich looking," he said.

I wanted to hear the longer description, but he had to hang up.

"You would have loved it" was one of the only personal sentences the boy had ever said to me.

He couldn't even call people by their first names. He carefully avoided saying my name for the first ten years I knew him. Whenever he said his cousin's name he sounded embarrassed, but sometimes he had no choice. When I brought this to his attention, he said, "I never use names."

"How come?" I asked.

He thought for a few seconds. "Too sentimental," he said.

"How do you communicate whom you're speaking to?" I said.

"I manage to get around it. Usually I succeed without resorting to saying the name."

Before we met, he didn't know about anything old. His parents lived in a modern house, now called contemporary, the kind of house they show on the HGTV channel, big houses in Arizona and California referred to as "homes" by the announcers. Couples were always buying "homes" on this program. "When they first saw it, the home was in disrepair" was a common theme of the "Restore America" part of the show. Couples would buy wrecked old houses and do them over, making them look worse in a new way. One woman said that she was looking for "pieces that addressed the theme of something like country charm." It was best to turn off the sound and just look at the houses.

The boy's family lived in one of the kinds of modern houses shown on HGTV even when they lived in Massachusetts, surrounded by big old homes. Anything they needed for their house had to be designed by an architect, even a lamp. A small cabinet took years to design and build.

He had no respect for antiques. On one occasion when we

went into an antiques store on Beacon Hill where I wanted to look at a striped velvet bench we saw in the window, the only thing he liked about it was the high price.

I thought the sentence, with the word "loved," was a turn for the better. But when I looked back on the tone of voice, I wasn't sure what it meant.

THE TWO THINGS

T HE NEXT TIME he called, I said I couldn't talk long but
that I'd call back in two hours. Whenever I called after making
this kind of plan, his phone would be turned off.

"Just tell me two things that make life worthwhile," he said
before agreeing to postpone the talk.

"If it's going to be that discussion again, we have to talk later
tonight," I said.

"See! You can't name two things," he said.

"Of course I can." I named the same old two things—work
and love. Then I said I had to get dinner together. "My husband
is pacing around eating a kind of white bread he likes to buy," I
said. "He'll eat the whole thing if we get into that subject."

During the last year, I'd burned pots of brown rice and vegetables and let spaghetti boil past al dente while talking to the
boy about the meaninglessness of life while my husband circled
around the room eating bread.

. . .

SOMEWHERE AMONG these conversations he had started to tell me this story:

"I saw the doctor in Philadelphia," he said. "I go in, the receptionist is behind a glass window. She has a Philadelphia accent. I give my name and say, 'I have an appointment.' There's this cheap copy of one of those sailboat paintings where the boat sticks out from the background—but it's like from a five-and-ten. It's an unbelievably bad reproduction."

Then before he could tell the next part, he had to hang up.

I was glad to hear the way he'd said his name. It seemed much better than my method of stumbling into doctors' offices—without remembering to say my name. I knew I'd be asked to repeat the last name and spell it, too, and I was tired of spelling it. I was tired of spelling my name and street address. Sometimes when someone spelled them both wrong, I'd go along with the new spellings just to simplify the process. In addition to this symptom, I didn't have the energy to chew lettuce in salad—both signs of something serious. I wished I'd changed my name to something really easy before the new uneducated generation grew up to be operators and receptionists. People—receptionists, phone operators, catalog-order takers—used to be able to understand names. Now the only catalog operators who understood names and addresses worked for the Vermont Country Store.

THE BOY had told me that he'd met the son of an illustrious photographer with the same last name as mine. The son was a college friend of his cousin's, and they'd met when the boy and his cousin were out walking around New York. The student was walking down the street with his girlfriend.

"There was something surprising about it I can't remember— either she was black . . . or she was fat. I know it was memorable in a surprising way," he'd said. "But now I can't remember which way."

He was interrupted by his mother, his father, or a call from his dealer on his cell phone.

DURING THAT week, the next time he answered the phone, he was in a rush.

"I'm off to the psychiatrist," he said in a happy way, too happy for the situation. Something was up. But what? I thought in the style of private detectives narrating plots in movies of the 1940s. "I'll call you later," he said.

"Will you really?" I asked. "Do you promise?"

"Yes," he said.

I CALLED the next day.

"I'm in a meeting," he said. "I'll call you later."

"Will you really?"

"Yes," he said.

"I'M WORRIED about that boy," I said to a narcissist acquaintance when we spoke on the phone on the night the boy said he was in a meeting. "He's not calling back."

"I know," she said. I heard sympathy in her voice, but she quickly switched subjects to how her skin looked. A lime blossom massage treatment gave her skin a glow. She liked to say this to her friends every day, maybe even several times a day.

I'd decided that I had a narcissistic personality disorder when I read about it in *The New York Times* in 1984. In my case this was combined or mixed in with a manic-depressive core. I'd read that Brian Wilson had been diagnosed as a manic-depressive-schizophrenic. I figured my own combination diagnosis probably did exist in psychiatry and was being tossed around by psychiatrists throwing terms together for lack of anything useful to do for patients and humanity in general.

But this acquaintance of mine was a plain narcissist. My condition was preferable, at least for others to be around, I thought narcissistically. Hers was better for her, keeping her from knowing or caring how her behavior appeared to other people.

We had one thing in common, which I'd discovered by accident: We both had the fear that we were borderline personalities. I didn't believe in these titles and had no respect for psychiatrists who used them in place of intelligence or skill, but one night I had overheard a psychiatrist showing off at a nearby table in a restaurant. I knew that psychiatrists like to give behavior a name and then apply to the name some medications they've learned from drug companies. He was describing the borderline personality to the civilians at his table.

The few doctors I knew socially—mainly the boy's father—didn't go parading medical terminology around at dinner. He, especially, had more entertaining subjects to talk about, and had people laughing when he said any sentence.

THE DEMON

The BOY'S FATHER had performed with this talent the night of the photo-book dinner. After the dinner, we'd all taken a bunch of taxis up to Washington Square. He sat squashed into the front passenger seat next to the Arab driver. The driver looked like the kind of man we see on the news rioting against our country. The boy's father had already told me that every New Year's Eve, at an annual dinner of surgeons, he was the one who predicted, "The greatest threat to world peace is extremist Muslim fundamentalism." But I was the one who always said the cabdrivers in Boston looked like Arab terrorists.

In the back so-called seat, I sat with my husband and, somehow, also my friend the now less-intoxicated landscape designer, and the boy, who was squeezed in somewhere too. People stand for this in New York—filthy, cramped taxis, all their knees crunched together into the hard back of the front seat. Yes, people love New York. They put up with it without mentioning the goings-on of this kind.

The cab ride took place before the worst era of turbaned drivers and the increasing evidence of their lowering standards of personal hygiene. But the regime of filthy cabs and drivers had been in place for a while and was in David Letterman's storage of jokes to use every week. It was before the world event that made everyone pretend to love everything about New York. Our taxi had the odor of cigarette butts and general dirtiness.

The surgeon said he had to fly off somewhere the next morning to give expert testimony at a malpractice trial. He started telling us about the last case in which he'd been called to give testimony.

Two doctors had been employed by a new multibillion-dollar fertility clinic. The condition of their employment was this: If they left the clinic before their two-year contract was up, they couldn't open their own clinic. "They're okay doctors, but in a year they quit and opened their own clinic," the surgeon said without surprise. He'd heard of everything.

A patient decided to sue one of the doctors after an expensive technological attempt at the clinic failed to result in pregnancy. One doctor ratted on the other doctor, and the facts of the ratting were these: The doctor in charge had placed the syringe of live embryos down on a table in order to say a prayer over it.

"They were some kind of Christian fundamentalists, and they believed that pregnancy couldn't be successful if the doctor doing the procedure was guilty of certain sins—adultery, stealing, murder, of course, homosexuality—probably being a Jew, too, but they didn't mention that," the surgeon said in his deep, knowing voice. His voice had a quality that seemed to show he knew about everything in the world—except that one thing, who Keith Richards was.

It turned out that one of the two doctors in the new clinic was actually known to be guilty of one of the sins, known around the clinic and the town.

The defense lawyer stood before the surgeon to question him. The surgeon told us, "The lawyer was a sixty-five-year-old short, fat Christian fundamentalist dressed in a brown suit with a brown vest, a white cowboy hat, and white cowboy boots. He had a head of thick white hair and wore a giant gold cross that hung around his neck, down over the brown vest.

"The lawyer said, 'You know, Doctor, about saying the prayer over the syringe of embryos?' I said, 'No, I don't know about any prayer.' 'Well, you know that a prayer is always said to keep the demons out of the embryo,' the lawyer said.

" 'I never heard of any demons getting into the embryo,' I said," the surgeon told us.

By then we were all laughing in the backseat. Each sentence made us laugh harder. The word "conniptions" was used for this kind of laughing at one time in the history of the world. By the time he said "demons getting into the embryo," someone was laughing so hard it sounded like crying. We were all wearing thick, sound-buffering winter coats, scarves, and gloves, so the hysteria was muffled.

As the surgeon continued in his serious, deep, and low voice, the group laughter reminded me of crying I'd heard before— quiet sobbing at funerals in cemeteries. The boy was silent and smiling—he'd heard the story before and he was watching his father's telling of it.

The gist of the case was a question: If the syringe of embryos was placed on a table for the time it took to say the prayer, would that hamper the chances of successful impregnation?

"The lawyer said, 'You know that the procedure is to place the syringe down on the table to say the prayer over it to prevent the demons from getting into the embryos?'

"I said, 'No, I don't know about any prayer.' Then he asked me, 'Do you believe in demons?' I said, 'No, I don't believe in demons.' And his next question was 'Then you don't believe that demons can get into the embryo?' I said, 'No, I don't believe that.'

"Then he tells me, 'Well, we're in the part of America that knows that there are demons and that they can get into the embryos if the doctor is a committer of adultery or other sins. Did you know that?'

"He held up a white flip chart with a list of the sins—the ten ways demons could get into the embryo. I said, 'No, I never heard that.' "

Then the surgeon was asked whether putting the syringe down on a table could weaken the embryos during the transfer.

" 'Well, maybe if they put it on a radiator, that would be bad,' I said. 'But not if they just put it down on a table for a minute.'

"I was dismissed," the surgeon said. "But first the lawyer said to me, 'Dr. Loquesto, you have a very strange way of thinking.'

"I said, 'There are millions of people on the East and West Coasts who think the same way.' Then I got out of town."

The whole time, I was worried about what the driver was thinking. I was always worried about what these Arab drivers were thinking, and time and history have proved that I was right to be worried. Then we were at Washington Square.

. . .

IN CONTRAST to the evening of the demon performance, when I returned home from the borderline-symptoms-description dinner, a few years later, I felt ill from hearing the description and how it might fit in with my life story.

I immediately drank some peppermint tea. Then the narcissist called to talk about a bamboo-lemongrass massage treatment. I told her my fear of the borderline diagnosis. "I'm afraid I'm one, too," she said, sounding disturbed by some secret knowledge.

We exchanged each symptom we knew of and said to each other, "You never do that," after each one. We tried to convince each other that we weren't borderline personalities, but because of her narcissism, she couldn't listen, and because of my narcissistic personality disorder, any bad description would fill up the place of emptiness. Inside the emptiness there was a magnet that attracted anything negative in the air and attached to it.

THE PHONE MESSAGE

T HERE WAS a message on my answering machine from the boy's father. He'd left his home phone number for me to call him back. I knew that the man, the world-renowned reproductive surgeon—professor, dean, and expert witness—would never be home on a weekday. It had to be something really serious for him to be away from work.

Maybe the boy was back in rehab, or this time in the hospital for an overdose—maybe in a coma, maybe in jail. I started to panic as these thoughts came speeding together while I pushed the buttons of the phone number. All these calls back and forth with the boy, and I had never figured out the speed dial.

His mother answered. I could tell from her voice that there was no time for chitchat. "I have a message to call Arnold," I said.

She said nothing but called him calmly, saying my name, "on line one." Whatever it was, she must have been all cried out.

His father said, "Hello." Just like that. Hello.

I said, "I have a message to call you." I knew I was saying it in a trembly voice.

But still, this is what his father said, and this is all:

"He killed himself." He said it in a shouting style. Not too loud. Lower than his usual shouting.

I tried to understand the sentence, but I couldn't. An empty space took over, and it quickly filled with those things the boy liked to discuss—love and pity. Love, pity, horror, and then the usual—disbelief.

I was using the wall phone in the kitchen. I found that I was bent over, leaning on the counter part of the old wall cabinet. In front of my eyes was a white antique bread box from 1930, but I couldn't quite see it. If I can't be outside, I always want to be looking out a window, but I forgot to move over to one. I stood leaned over, facing the bread box filled with vitamin bottles.

Into the silence I heard his father say my name with a question mark, as if he thought I'd fainted, or even died.

HE WAS another one who avoided addressing people by their first names, and when referring to anyone in the third person, including women, he used only last names, as a form of disrespect for all human beings, especially female ones. But on the day of this news, when I couldn't speak, he said my name again, this time with an urgent medical sound. The only feelings I'd ever heard in his voice before this were impatience and anger.

"Yes," I said.

"Are you there?" he said.

Was I there? Not exactly. I was nowhere, vanished, dissolved, completely gone from the human form I'd previously inhabited.

"I have to call you back," I said. "I can't talk right now."

"Why not?" he said matter-of-factly.

"Because I can't believe it," I said. I started to cry as I said the sentence. The crying didn't sound as if it would go with talking.

"But it's true," he said.

"It was an accident," I said. By then I was crying hard enough to have embarrassed my friend the boy. But as I pictured him and heard the words "it's true," I cried harder. I cared about him even more, along with all the sentences I'd heard him say since he was eleven, and the sadness of his whole life. With that came the thought of how he must have felt during the last weeks of his life.

I thought I had defended myself against this kind of crying after my mother died and then my father. And, before that, President Kennedy, Robert Kennedy, and Elvis Presley. That was it. I'd used it up. I was dead myself—inside, anyway. I was the walking dead.

The boy's father continued saying words to me in a cold-hearted style he'd learned in medical school and then practiced throughout his career.

"It wasn't an accident," he said. "He bought a rope."

He named the method of suicide. "It was premeditated. He was a heroin addict. He loved heroin. He couldn't give it up. He knew I'd get the credit card bill with the cash withdrawals soon. He'd have to go back to rehab. He'd rather be dead. Now he is."

Now he is, I tried thinking. "He didn't mean to do it," I said in between crying and speaking. "He loved life."

"He didn't love life!" his father said, ready to argue. "He loved heroin."

"He was entertained by life," I said in a state of remembering what that meant. "He was interested in everything," I tried to say. "He couldn't end his life."

"He did end it. We went out to dinner. He was in a good mood. He told stories. We came home and he went upstairs. I went up ten minutes later and I found him."

Every word he said was a blow. Not just to me but a triple blow, as I pictured it, to him and the boy's mother, too. Especially her. No, both of them. The scene, the calling of 911. Every word made me cry harder. Then I couldn't stand hearing the crying. The sound of it shocked me and spread the heartbreak around and out into the room.

I felt sorry for the boy's father, having to listen. But underneath the cruel seconds of the moments, I was realizing that he liked listening to it. He didn't interrupt. He took it in. He needed it. He was a man who needed women to cry in his place, like designated drivers or proxy voters. There must be men who need women around for expressions of all the feelings they can't manage for themselves. It was like one of those book titles— *Men Who Can't Cry and the Women Who Cry for Them.*

"I tried to resuscitate him," he said in his matter-of-fact way.

"Did you call 911?" I asked in my pitiful state of seeing the scene and trying not to see it at the same time. I had somehow moved into the living room, where I leaned on the back of an old armchair slipcovered with faded pink flowers on a spilled-tea-colored background. The chair seemed too beautiful to be used this way. I was looking through the French doors out to the trees and the empty sky as I asked my pathetic questions.

When the design of the roses was printed on the fabric, I couldn't help thinking, when these particular flowers were chosen long ago in England—when the designers assembled to choose this rose and this green for the leaves—when discussions took place over this shade of pink or that—did anyone imagine their faded old roses would end up on a chair here in the USA, where the drug laws are such that a precocious boy would become a drug addict, buy heroin in the street, give up on his life, and buy a rope and kill himself in his parents' house in Beverly Hills, and that one of his remaining friends, a hollowed-out person without a soul, would lean on the rose-covered chair and look out the window and cry?

Only the loveliest plans must have been envisioned for the flower-printed linen on the curved arm of the beautiful old chair. But probably the British know all the terrible things in life that can happen on their rose-covered chairs and they take them in stride.

"I CALLED 911," his father said. "I tried to save him myself. It was too late. He was gone."

I couldn't get the word "rope" out of my mind, or into it, either. I thought of the Alfred Hitchcock movie *Rope*, a creepy and least-favorite one I could never watch through to the end.

"It was an accident," I had to say again. I was pleading, I was begging. "He meant to be found," I begged.

"Maybe," his father said. He sounded tired. Tired and sad.

"He was unique," I said, remembering the ways in which he was. Then I felt the beginning of giving up. "He was out of this world," I said most pathetically.

"That, he was. All those things. But now he's gone."

"How could this happen?" I said as I tried out believing the facts.

"He thought the world was a terrible place," his father said.

"It is," I said. "But he was always working on a way to avoid the most terrible part."

"Well, he found a way now," his father said in that low, deep style he had.

During this conversation I was understanding the meaning of the word "brokenhearted." Because when you cry that hard, you can feel the sensation of the heart physically splitting apart and breaking into pieces inside the chest. There must be a medical explanation of how that works, I thought. It must take its toll on the organ. I made a mental note to look it up if it didn't kill me right then.

In my brain I heard the sentence "He thought the world was a horrible place"—it was what Teresa Wright says about her uncle Charlie, Joseph Cotten, the strangler, at the end of the movie, when she tries to explain his criminal behavior to herself and to the detective she's fallen in love with—and he with her, as the boy liked to say. "He thought the world was a horrible place. He couldn't have been very happy ever, he didn't trust people, he hated them, he hated the whole world," she says.

"The whole world's hell, what does it matter what happens in it?" he says to her.

Those who find the world a horrible place—some must kill others, some themselves. But the boy hadn't watched the end of the movie that night. The drug had knocked him out and put him to sleep.

And what bad manners, I thought in my narcissistic-personality mode, to promise to call back, to confide, to listen and advise, and then to do this. He took me to the brink with him, then he jumped off. How rude.

ETIQUETTE COURSE

I HAD RECOMMENDED he take an etiquette course to help him feel confident and act smooth with the aristocratic class with whom he wished to socialize when he got to college and found out about the Upper East Side. "Sounds like a good idea," he said. He didn't know what etiquette was before I explained. Once, at dinner in his parents' home, he'd reached all the way across the table to get a basket of bread. He didn't know about not reaching.

"You'll feel more confident and your social path will be more streamlined," I told him. I didn't mention the bread incident, a minuscule one in the background of his generally all-spooky behavior.

If that hadn't worked, at least he would have learned some better manners and prepared for this last act in a more considerate way.

I had a copy of *Letitia Baldrige's Complete Guide to the New*

Manners for the '90s, but I didn't remember any advice on suicide planning.

After a few minutes of this conversation with the boy's father, the same conversation over and over in different versions, we were finished with all the ways we could say the same things. He took advantage of the break to say something else, on the next part of the subject.

I wasn't thinking ahead of the moments we were in, because we seemed unreal and outside life and time, like cutout paper-doll people pasted onto a page. In addition to other disorders, I had the obsessive-compulsive disorder. I could have stayed stuck for an hour on that pasted page.

But there was the next thing: "We're not having a funeral for him," his father said.

The word "funeral"—I couldn't think of this word in association with the boy. "For him" had an additional cruel sound. I was glad to hear the word "funeral" quickly undone by the word "not" before it was uttered. I was getting more shocks from this new line of thought and all I could say was "Oh," as I kept crying. I asked no questions. I wanted no answers. Don't have a funeral—good—because that will keep it in the realm of unhappening, was my reasoning.

The boy had recently mentioned the word to me in an unfeeling and chatty way.

"Did you hear about my grandmother?" he'd said.

I said I knew she'd been in what's called failing health for some time. "I haven't heard anything lately," I said. "Is it the worst?"

"Yes," he said. "Except it's really for the best at this stage."

He used to describe her attempts to settle a family dispute

over an inherited lamp. "Every night after dinner she says to the sixty-year-old nephew, 'Now, Edward, about the lamp.' "

"It's too bad people can't live a long time in good health and then wear out and fade away in peace the way they do in Okinawa and some other islands," I said as I thought of his grandmother.

"Yes," he said. "But our comical monkey bodies dictate otherwise."

I was admiring his sentence, so I laughed with an extra bonus of appreciation for his talent.

HE'D MASTERED a combination—coldness and weariness, resulting from heroin use. He mentioned going to the funeral as if he were going out to buy a new cell phone.

His grandmother knew enough to be worried about him when he was twelve. She said he was like a fifty-year-old man the way he walked aimlessly through the room with his hands in his pockets while jingling the change around inside the pockets. She smiled, but behind the smile, or above it, in the area of the eyes, she was worried, and she said the boy's grandfather didn't think being precocious was a completely good thing. The grandfather was known for his wisdom, but by the time I met him, he was sitting and playing solitaire at the kitchen table while eating fruit salad.

"I was reading the evening paper," the boy had said to me when he was twelve. I told this to his grandmother and she laughed, but not wholeheartedly. Good that she wasn't around for the last activities he'd gotten into.

"WHO'S THERE with you?" I asked the boy's father.

"No one. Just us," he said.

"Just you two?" I tried to see them alone together in their large house with this having happened.

"Yes. Some people were here, but they left."

"What will you do now? Are your relatives coming?" I said.

"I don't know yet. We have to go to Philadelphia."

I asked why. I didn't know what I was asking.

And then he said in his dark, low voice, "I have to bury him."

Another part of the subject I wasn't following. There was no future for me in the conversation if it was going to go this way.

"I can't talk about this," I said.

"Why not? We have to face it."

"I'm not good at facing things," I said.

"Well, okay, we'll talk to you later. I'll call you."

"Is there any way I can be of help?" I asked, with that etiquette book in the background, but I didn't know what I meant.

"Not now," he said. "There's nothing left to do."

AFTER THE PHONE MESSAGE

S HOULD I TAKE a Xanax? Should I drink thirty drops of valerian in an ounce of warm water? Should I take half of a Klonopin? Should I eat a peach? They weren't in season yet, at least
the organically grown white ones, and regular peaches were on
Dr. Andrew Weil's list of the dirty dozen most pesticide-sprayed
fruits.

I'll have to stop crying at some point, so I should stop now, I
thought. Because outside, in my workroom, I had no assistant to
come and organize papers. My former assistants used to come
and do everything wrong, partly on purpose and partly unconsciously, in the style of passive-aggressive experts.

The assistants would stay in the workroom, mixing things
up, misfiling papers, writing with cheap mechanical pencils
they'd ordered by the boxload so that their spindly writing in
the light, thin pencil lead would be illegible. They'd put cards in
the Rolodex without phone numbers, or write phone numbers

without addresses, write names of people without the names of their businesses, or businesses without the names of anyone who worked there. Or one of their favorite techniques was to take contact sheets and negatives and pile them together under catalogs from Office Max, phone books, and sheets of bubble wrap, old copies of *Vegetarian Times*, and requests for money from Doctors Without Borders. It was all the same to them.

The papers never moved off the desk. The clock never got a new battery. It was always one o'clock during the years they worked there.

I SHOULD wash my face, splash water on it without looking in the mirror. I expected the face would look like one of those inflatable red rubber pancakes used for physical therapy, exercise, or swim therapy. I'd been told by a facialist hundreds of times that Paul Newman put his whole face into a bowl of ice water when he got up in the morning.

I had only this one day to get organized without an assistant's help, or hindrance, because I had only four days to pack up and leave for the summer. I had to go on a work project for *Look at the Moon*—photographs of the sky and other natural wonders visible only on that island. And I'd be staying in the rented house where the boy had first called me the summer before to say he wasn't a drug addict.

Any friends of mine who'd met him were all at pressure-filled jobs and it would be bad manners to call them with this news.

At an antique-folk-art show on a New York pier in the 1980s I saw a wooden man-statue once used outside a men's haberdashery store in 1920. The man was an idea of a man, not a real man—the blue suit, the tie, the white shirt, the decent face many men had before our society became filled with the thugs and goons David Letterman mentioned while speaking to Letitia Baldrige the time she appeared on his show in order to promote her book. The men I knew were like that wooden man.

Didn't I know any females I could speak to? The narcissist—I didn't dare disturb her during the day. She'd be busy with crises connected to sending a cake to her son at boarding school.

I thought of a plan. I'd prepare people: I'd say, "heroin addict," "in and out of rehab," "getting more desperate"—and they'd guess. I wouldn't have to batter them down with the cruelest words.

I'D NEVER had a professional assistant. When I first laid eyes on one at her main place of employment—a medical complex, office structure, or bungalow-barracks—she was hanging over a porch rail with a can of soda in her hand. From her appearance I thought that she must be a patient, or a relative waiting for a patient, but because of the proprietary air she had of belonging to the building-bungalow-barracks, it was clear that she had some rights there.

These rights were hers, I discovered, because she was the assistant for the entire barracks—six different kinds of "medical professional" offices. This most outlandish place is where I'd been referred for psychotherapy.

I accepted this setup, and continued on at the establishment, in spite of it, for a year of appointments.

The doctor I saw had mentioned that he had never smoked—that was reason enough for me to sign on there. This was the place to which my friend the boy had referred when he said, "I advise you never to go back there. It's unprofessional."

The same day I saw the manager hanging over the rail with the soda can, I witnessed a more unbelievable display of behavior in the immediate vicinity of the medical bungalow.

It was a hot day in June, but this place wasn't far from the water, so a breeze almost blew and kept the heat down in the area, which was surrounded by fields and farms. That was why I went back there—location—weather, fresh air, green grass, wildflower meadows, unobstructed by high buildings and all that went with building life.

Outside the bungalow office a workman was painting the green trim of the windows. The man was big and hefty. He wore blue jeans, workman style and roomy—lucky for everyone that they were roomy. He wore a tight sleeveless white T-shirt, showing tattoos on his arms. His large midsection and back were partially exposed in the style made famous by Dan Aykroyd on *Saturday Night Live,* and I thought I spied some tattoo parts on the back area, too, before I looked away. Around his head he wore a yellow bandanna tied over long dark hair and he was smoking a cigarette.

A short, stocky fellow approached him—I assumed he was the contractor; he was dressed in regular khaki pants and a plaid sport shirt. He gave the worker some instructions and then said in a voice everyone could hear, "Don't be depressed. I'll try to get you some money." Then the stocky, short man entered the building through the medical door. Seeing this was worth the trip there no matter how the appointment might turn out.

I was waiting outside in the hot air for the doctor because there was no ventilation in the waiting room, which smelled of toxic fumes and was filled with drug-company advertising brochures and the worst magazines known to mankind.

Some months later, I pointed out the collection of periodicals to the doctor.

"Yes, well, but how many people would read *The New York Review of Books* if we had it out here?" he'd said as he straightened out copies of magazines without taking note of the cover lines with the words HOTTER this and that, and even more.

The short man came out again. He looked at me and said, "Hello!" in a salacious manner. Since my forties were almost completely over, I wasn't used to the look or voice, and when I got home, I stood in front of a mirror to see what he might have meant. It must have been this: My linen skirt was old and washed thin, and a day like that one was too hot for a slip. Through the thin skirt, once light-green, by then faded almost to white, my two legs were completely visible.

The next day I went to the one underwear store in the whole town. I bought the thinnest cotton half-slip available and wore it under the skirt, although the two layers of fabric were too hot for the globally warmed-up days. On my next trip to a hot place I stopped near an abandoned farm and, while in the car, took the slip off and used a small scissors from a glove-compartment sewing kit to cut off a section from the knees down.

When I got into the psychiatrist's office, he had the window open, since the air-conditioning wasn't working right, or so he claimed—people use this alibi for all kinds of reasons. Smoke from the cigarette of the worker, who was still painting the windows, was blowing directly into the office.

"I smell cigarette smoke," I said to the doctor.

"No one is smoking in here," he said.

I told him about the outside situation. "I'll go right out and tell him he must stop immediately!" the doctor said. He leapt up from his chair as if he wanted to get outside and breathe some air himself.

When he returned, I told him what I'd heard spoken between the tattooed one and the stocky one.

"Well," he said, and slowly, as if each word had weight and significance: "The . . . contractor . . . is . . . also . . . a . . . therapist." Then he smiled and started to laugh, as if he thought it was one of the funniest things he'd ever heard.

"You mean he works here—doing both jobs?" I said.

"Yes, he does," the doctor said.

Then I started to laugh. I couldn't believe I had stumbled into this place of delectable unprofessionalism.

"See, you don't know all the things we have going on here," he said with a mad smile.

I couldn't know then that this madness with the psychiatrist would lead to the edge of insanity, or that one day the boy and I would discuss that we'd both been referred to the same sanatorium in Massachusetts.

"At least we'd have each other to talk to," I'd said to the boy when we realized we might be in the same place someday, maybe soon.

"But I'd be in the drug part and you'd be in the psychiatric part," he'd said. "I was there. I know." Whenever he said the word "drug" in reference to himself, he said it really quietly.

"But isn't fraternizing between the wards permitted?" I asked.

"I don't think so," he said. "The drug part is like a prison. So that's that," he said with a sigh. "I advise you not to go."

. . .

WHEN I thought back to the day of the phone call, I thought I had splashed water on my face, or maybe I hadn't.

I remembered that I opened the door and went out to my workroom. The cleaning helper was there. I'd forgotten about her.

"You know about my friend the recovering heroin addict?" I said to her. "He killed himself."

I guess she'd heard this kind of thing before. She didn't show any surprise. She kept right on working, moving piles of paper around from here to there. "Where?" was always the question after she left, always in a hurry to get to an Italian-named macaroni store on the highway before it closed—she'd said so.

"This is what they do. This is what happens with a lot of them," she said as I told her a fact or two. She didn't look up at me from the stacks of paper. Now he was just one of "them." He was no longer the person he'd been.

HOW DID THIS HAPPEN?

I KNEW THAT I had to stop thinking about him as an eleven-year-old boy, the way he was when I first met him on a hot day in New England. His father had introduced us in his super-speedy way. He was in a rush to a meeting of thirty reproductive surgeons in his living room. I was there to photograph the thirty, and the surgeon dashed upstairs to his room-size closet to change out of his suit jacket. The boy was hanging about idly, having done his easy homework hours before. He stared at me, appearing to take in my whole life story in an instant.

"You two are going to get along great!" his father had said in a shouting style intended to convey something uncomplimentary. The under-meaning was, You're both weird in the same way.

After that, the boy put a leash on his dog and we walked around outside the house discussing which state had the higher rate of Lyme disease, Connecticut or Massachusetts. The boy was dressed as if his mother had chosen his clothing, in khaki

Bermuda shorts and a polo shirt—luckily for all of us, it was minus the polo player—and he wore Top-Sider moccasins. This was before he cared much about how he looked. His shorts were wrinkled and his polo shirt hung out at a lopsided angle. His thick, wavy Jeff Chandler hair was messed up and standing out in a few directions. I noticed during the evening that his little legs were child-thin and shaped like his mother's legs, although a slight chubbiness was threatening his midsection and making his polo shirt hang in the crooked way.

When I waved good-bye to him outside in the dark driveway where he'd stood nonstop lecturing on the history of the kinds of cars his parents owned then, and all the years before, I noticed his little knobby knees below the bottom of his shorts. The messed-up hair, the slightly buck teeth, the deadpan expression, the shirt askew over the baggy shorts, and the thin, delicate legs with the round knees—seeing this was the beginning of my attachment to him and his sad and lonely place in his family and the world.

NEXT, I'D seen him at a most awkward event in his life, a religious celebration he'd been forced to have for his thirteenth birthday. This embarrassed him, since his plan was to join the conservative Christian Republican world. When he told me this plan at a later age—sixteen—I said, "The religious ceremony of your birthday celebration was videotaped."

"No one has it but us," he said.

"The FBI could have a copy," I said.

"How? How could they?" he asked. "No agents were present," he said. But he sounded worried.

He wore a little white tuxedo, again conjured up by his mother, and he was sitting at a table with a bunch of thirteen-year-old kids, all staring straight ahead without smiling or speaking.

At the end of the night's toned-down festivities, the boy was pressed into several family-picture-taking episodes by a professional photographer. During this part of the event, my husband and I were taking our leave. I looked back at the boy, who had on his pre-existential expression of good-natured cooperation mixed with the beginnings of the disdain to come, and I waved and smiled in a moment of empathy. To my surprise he smiled back. The smile had a second of happiness in it, meaning, "Isn't this ridiculous?" or, "It's almost over." He did look a little like Alfred E. Neuman, and he didn't mind.

I HAD to learn to see him as a college boy/heroin addict. I had missed this whole stage of his development.

"I saw him decline," his cousin told me. "It was like a serious, fatal illness. It wasn't a surprise. I watched it for four years. He looked like a Holocaust victim. He never ate food. He had black circles under his eyes. The drug therapist told us afterwards that he'd used drugs every single day the last year of his life."

I KNEW no spiritual counselors. Or any counselors. I knew no one to talk to at all, now that the boy was gone from the world.

I looked at the valerian tincture and I looked at the Xanax, both in a basket of vitamins on the kitchen table. I'd never taken a pill for daytime problems, but this would be a good time to start.

I thought of asking someone for an opinion, but whoever I asked would probably say, "There's no pill for this."

. . .

I CALLED a medical professor who was a friend of the boy's father and whole family. He sounded glad when he answered the phone, because the last time we'd met was at a fun-filled event.

The surgeon's friend hadn't an inkling of what he was about to hear.

I practiced the technique I'd been preparing.

"Did you know he was a heroin addict?" I said.

"No," he said.

Then I told the story, and as I did, I heard his voice getting ready for the end. The silence, the pause, the yes. By the time I got there, he already knew.

When he called back later, he said, "They're cloistered at home. They don't want to see or talk to anyone."

MEDICATION AND work were all I had for the day—maybe the rest of my life. I might end up like Jacqueline Kennedy's cousin, the younger Edie Beale—if I was lucky. I'd visited her abandoned garden many times, before and after its restoration. In both conditions it was twenty times the size of ours, and filled with flowers, trees, shrubs, old walls, fences, and vines. I would end up even worse without this kind of a garden for solace and peace.

ON THAT afternoon, the day after the boy ended his life, the hardware-store manager called to inform me that there were no two-line cordless phones in the whole town. They love to give this kind of information. Because if there were such a phone, they might be asked to go to the stockroom and find one.

In the midst of this situation, the UPS man arrived with a box from J&R Music World. I didn't remember having ordered

anything. I tore open the box with pruning shears. Inside was a
two-line cordless phone, a silver phone the boy had advised me
to order the week before. "Get the GigaRing," he said. "It's the
best one if you can't spend six hundred dollars on a really good
one."

There it was. I opened the box and looked at the phone. I
touched it. You little jerk, I thought about my friend the boy,
now we can't even criticize the phone together—I was alone
with the grotesque object. I wanted to know how he could have
talked me into buying this phone at the same time he was planning his suicide.

I threw it, box and all, onto the washing machine in the laundry room. Then I turned around and leaned on the dryer and
cried in a new way I didn't want anyone to hear. It would be too
much of a burden to anyone, even the birds I heard chirping
outside. The sound of opening a window or turning a doorknob
could scare them away.

The expensive high-tech silver stand-up receiver—I'd never
knowingly order such a thing. It was one of his delusions of
grandeur to recommend the phone. And on top of that, it wasn't
all silver, it was part black and he knew that I wanted nothing
black in my sight, but he tried to train me out of the phobia for
the purposes of technology. The phone had the special name,
and phones with names were things he knew about.

I hoped I wouldn't be getting any mail from him when I saw
he could still reach me with a phone. The purpose of this phone
was to enable me to do many things out of normal phone range
while talking to him as long as he wanted.

I looked around. I didn't even have a cat, I remembered. A cat
could be there annoying us and getting in the way. A dog would

be more understanding. That's what Andrew Weil had written about dogs, and I believed everything he said, except the part about garlic—that if you eat it all the time it doesn't cause a garlic odor.

THE WEEKEND was a time of hot, humid nothingness.

"What's wrong?" my husband asked a few times. I'd already told him the news, which he was able to forget right away.

I reminded him: "My close friend committed suicide. I'm thinking about him."

I had to learn that men were a kind of nonhuman species; they were like beings from outer space who needed a form of simple communication. I'd seen this in science fiction movies— earthlings trying to talk to robots and beings from other planets. When I tried it out, it worked and kept down the expectations. Men weren't like actual human beings, and I'd proceed accordingly. I hadn't read the *Men Are from Mars* book, but I understood the principle behind it.

Anyone who called got the story. Soon I was tired of it— "heroin," "rehab," the last phone calls. People didn't like the story and soon I stopped bothering them with it. I could tell that some people thought it was bad manners for me to tell them.

The narcissist was a special case. I left a message for her the first night. "Something really bad has happened with the boy."

She called back right away. On other occasions she might take a week or a month to return a call—calling only when she was in the mood to talk about recipes or shampoo. I had a two-minute tolerance in my brain for these subjects.

She owned an art gallery near San Francisco where she showed paintings depicting accidents and disasters. She'd guessed the ending from my message and wanted to talk about it all night. Like most of my friends, she took antianxiety medication, and the talking had to take place before the medicine kicked in. The time-zone difference made it even more difficult for us.

All of my friends had this in common—we'd never taken any psychomedication until we were forty-four or -five. We did it as a last resort, pressured by doctors. The whole psychiatric profession was probably sick and tired of hearing problems and just wanted everyone to take pills and shut up. My more well mannered friends would say, "The Klonopin," "Ambien," "Xanax," or even two of the three, "kicked in. I can't think straight," or, "I have to go to sleep before it wears off."

A psychiatrist had warned me about this a couple of years before. "If you keep doing one more thing, you'll miss the opportune moment for sleep," he'd said. He knew I had that compulsion to do more and more things at night, things like laundry and recycling, and he said that he had the same compulsion.

"I guess your analysis was a failure," I said.

"A partial failure," he'd agreed. "One continues to struggle," he said, one of his favorite ways of excusing his faults.

I disregarded his advice and always kept doing the one more thing. I hadn't really slept since 1983.

He'd told me the advice specifically about Ambien, but the one time I tried that drug the sleep it produced wasn't real sleep.

I'd read a description of the topic in an early story by Marcel Proust:

"The feebleness one experiences several minutes before sleep induced by a bromide. Suddenly perceiving nothing, no dream, no sensation, between his last thought and this one . . . 'What? I haven't slept yet?' But then seeing it was broad daylight, he realized that for over six hours he had been possessed by bromidic sleep."

The boy and I had once agreed about this, both saying into the phone at the same time, "I hate Ambien!" His father used to yell, "I hate Harold Pinter!" the same way whenever I recommended *The Birthday Party*.

The boy said Ambien didn't help him sleep at all, and when he'd told his doctor, the doctor said, "Take two more. Take six."

All of us in the anxiety club knew about seizing the moment for sleep, but some would keep talking; they'd make no sense and fall asleep talking.

I'd say, "Let's talk tomorrow," or, "Let's go to sleep," or, "Your medicine has taken effect." And they'd say, "No, let's talk now," as they fell asleep.

These are my friends, I'd think. This is where I am.

The day after the boy ended his life, I realized that I might have been on the phone talking about him when he was committing this act.

I should have kept calling him, not talking to my friends about why he wasn't calling back. This is the flaw of many women, I was learning—talking instead of acting. I should have told him again the answer to his request "Tell me two things that make life worthwhile." I should have told him right then instead of postponing the talk. I should have quickly made up a list of more things.

But maybe he'd turned the phone off once he'd made up his mind. But maybe in haste he'd left it on and he would have seen the vibration feature of the phone in his jacket pocket.

Just the thought of his jacket was unbearable—his jackets, which were so important to him in high school. He'd shown me how he'd organized his closet in his room at home when he was fifteen. All the jackets hung neatly with big spaces between them. He explained which jacket was for which purpose: one for school, one for lectures, one for dinners out, one for dinner parties. He tried on one or two and walked around. Some of the jackets were hand-me-downs—one from his father, a navy pea coat from college. One was black faux fur, from a cousin.

"Don't wear that one," I'd said.

"But it's warm," he said, "for the icy-cold weather when I go to night classes in Cambridge."

"It looks like something Liberace wore," I said. "You should get rid of it."

"I'll bring it back down to the basement storage closet," he said.

The sport coats were of greatest importance to him, especially his navy blue blazers. They gave him the most investment-banker confidence. A khaki one had a slight safari look. I suggested that he bring that to the basement while he was making the trip down there.

Then I asked if he would come to our house and organize our three closets.

"People have requested this of me before," he said. "You'd have to agree to get rid of eighty percent of everything."

I agreed, because our closets were down to twenty percent already. The problem wasn't the clothing but the tiny closets in the old house. Things fell onto one another and onto the floor.

There was one shelf in my closet. Nothing fit onto the shelf but an old torn white nightgown.

"Our house was built during the Depression," I explained.

"That can be a problem," he said. "Why doesn't your husband

try to make more money?" the boy asked when he thought about the closets. "He's in the real world."

"We forgot about money," I said. "We were from the sixties."

"He could have made money afterwards. And you could take photos in Hollywood."

I explained that in the sixties people didn't know how much money would be necessary to live decently in modern times. But that discussion led to feeling middle-aged, so we changed the subject to Mel Tormé. He led me over to his two hundred Mel Tormé CDs and LPs.

I pointed out the small pudgy hands of the singer on one of the CD covers. I'd never looked carefully at the man before.

As I took in the overall appearance of Mel Tormé, I said, "Maybe you like him because he's the same physical type as your father."

"You think?" the boy said, willing to consider this seriously.

Then I said, "No, he looks something like a gay guy."

The boy didn't agree. But he managed to say, "I never noticed his hands."

Usually he noticed everything. He sounded surprised that something like pudgy hands could have gone right by him. When he was twelve he told me about a man his father knew. "The man has an apple-shaped head on a body of long sticks. He's Greek. He dresses in all different shades of blue—light, dark, all clashing with each other. Even his hat is blue. He wears them all together."

WHEN HE was fourteen, he'd told me about a physics professor he'd met at a party he attended with his parents in Cambridge. I'd met the man once or twice. He said this about the man: "He's a depressed upper-middle-aged man with nothing to look forward to in his diminishing career. At parties he becomes more morose." Then he asked, "Did you ever notice how his teeth are all slanted towards each other and pointed to the back of his mouth?" I said no.

"He's going through some kind of serious breakdown where he talks about the dumplings his mother cooked when he was a boy—that and the striped mittens she knitted for him. He's almost crying when he gets to the dumplings and the mittens. No one knows what to do about him at the university."

In a phone call the same year, he'd described another party: "You go in, there's one lamp in the whole huge living room. The hors d'oeuvres are a tiny potato on a toothpick. They're both doctors, the hosts, but she's the more ambitious one. He does the housework and takes their kids places."

They let the boy go into the kitchen and see all the other trays of food. "They had these little meringue dessert cakes and I happen to love meringue," he said. "Do you?"

"You know how I feel about eggs or animal products of any kind."

"It's egg whites, I thought," he said.

"The idea of the egg, not just the health part," I said.

"Well, I suggest it would be worth your while to get over that and try some meringue," he said. "They told me I could have all the leftover meringue cakes to take home. So we're leaving with the box of cakes and I just want to get home and get it into the refrigerator before the meringue melts into the dough, but the mentally collapsed professor is still telling me about the mittens his mother knitted for him."

"It sounds so sad. Don't you feel sorry for him?" I said.

"Not really. Those crooked inward-pointing teeth are too distracting for me to really pay attention."

"What will happen to him?" I asked.

"No one knows. They all have their own problems. The doctor husband of the ambitious doctor wife is sitting in a chair drinking and singing Irish songs to himself, his face lit by the one lamp in the whole dark, potato-filled room."

"There must have been some other hors d'oeuvres besides potatoes on toothpicks," I said. "Maybe there was another ingredient on the toothpicks you couldn't see."

"No, believe me, it was just a potato on a toothpick," he said. "I swear."

They gave him another big box of meringues as he left. "They were, like, 'Would you want some of the hors d'oeuvres, too?' And we're all, like, 'Thank you, we've had too many as it is.' "

NOT ELVIS PRESLEY

H E LOOKS PUDGY and unhealthy," I said when I studied the Mel Tormé CD covers. "He should change his diet and get some exercise."

"You think that's a toupee?" the boy asked.

"That or a bad spray style," I said.

He didn't care about that or the pudginess. "The Velvet Fog, he's called," he said. "Don't you agree?"

"Well, you know how much I love Elvis Presley. They're opposites," I said.

"I forgot about that," the boy said. "But it's an obsession of another order."

When I pictured his little jacket with the phone in the pocket, I would sink down into the black abyss of thought.

Maybe he was so nihilistic he would have enjoyed ignoring the phone vibration in those last moments of his life. That was one of the thoughts.

But his jacket wasn't little anymore. He had grown to be five-foot-ten and had such good posture that he looked even taller. Unlike some guys who are five-foot-ten and insist they are six-foot-two or ones with bad posture who look five-foot-eight.

The list of loss, including and especially Elvis Presley, was growing. Also on my mind I had an additional list, of other people I didn't personally know whose passing I couldn't accept, starting with Buddy Holly, Roy Orbison, Ricky Nelson, John Lennon, Otis Redding, Peter Sellers, Andy Kaufman, Jacqueline Kennedy, John Candy, Princess Diana, and Joseph Heller. The final, most recent Kennedy was completely unacceptable to many, who haven't faced it to this day.

WE LEFT for our trip as if nothing had happened.

THE SAME KITCHEN
IN NANTUCKET

Sometimes there would be a message on the machine from the boy's father, calling from his office at the medical school. Sometimes there would be more than one message. In California three-thirty was his phone hour, but it was six-thirty in Nantucket, when there was the best of the last light shining on everything.

The boy had left a list of people to notify in the event of his death. "You're on the list," his father told me. He said he'd had to call the people on the list in addition to calling relatives and friends.

"They all say they have to hang up and that they'll call back. I don't let them hang up. I want to hear what they say about him."

"Maybe they need time to collect themselves," I said.

"I don't care. I don't want to wait. I want to hear it right then."

All day the doctor performed surgeries, taught fellows, gave lectures, and helped people bring babies into this world, where the babies could grow up and become addicts. The time span from babyhood to drug addiction now seemed to me to pass in a few years. I knew how busy the doctor was, and if he called more than once, it meant I had to call him back no matter what the light was outside.

Every time I talked to him, he had a new mood. Sometimes he was angry and said he hated his dead son. "I'm cutting him out of my life," he'd say. "He was selfish to do this to us all. I'm going to forget all about him."

"He didn't know what he was doing," I said. I told him that I'd read that heroin addicts had opiate molecules clinging to their brains.

"How long does it stay in the body?" he asked.

"You're the doctor," I said. "I don't know any medical facts."

In the days when I'd first gone to photograph the surgeon in his hospital, we were walking across an interior bridge that connected an old part of the hospital to a new modern wing. The bridge wasn't as hideous as others I came across later on, for example, the one in Boston connecting a department store to a mangled nest of steel and concrete—other stores—what's known as a mall.

Yet at the surgeon's hospital, as we crossed the interior bridge in the afternoon light, I saw that gardens had been planted outside—not the best gardens, but mound-shaped gardens of santolina and other clumps of light green, mixed with medium green, and rocks and what appeared to be desert flowers. How did some landscape designer get anything as good as this approved, I wondered as we walked along and the aroma of institutional food from the hospital cafeteria wafted up to the bridge. I'd seen the food with my own eyes: creamed soup, American cheese, canned fruit with Jell-O under plastic domes, cottage cheese, and even maraschino cherries.

"I wish I could work here," I said to the surgeon as I looked out at the green plants. I'd never worked in a place where intelligent, white-coated women and men worked hard and said friendly things to one another all day in long corridors. Two researchers were making popcorn in a lab I passed by one afternoon. Most likely they were having an affair in a broom closet somewhere nearby.

When I said I'd like to work there, the surgeon said, "Go speak to the dean."

"But I have no medical knowledge," I said.

"That hasn't stopped him before," the surgeon said.

I'd heard a research doctor ask a lab technician to come see his slides of something, and when I asked the surgeon who the man was, he said, "We *think* he's a doctor. We're not sure."

"How can that be?" I asked.

"He's not allowed to see patients," the surgeon said.

I SHOULDN'T stay in these conversations, I'd think as I saw the light changing outside the window. They were bad for both of us, I could tell. Every angry word he said did some damage. By then I'd read the book titled *Anger Kills*, but maybe the surgeon was the exception to the rule. Maybe his anger could kill me and leave him fine. The boy had told me that his father didn't even know his own cholesterol. When I asked the surgeon about this, he said, "Why do I need to know?"

THE NIHILIST CHEFS

W HENEVER I TOLD my husband what the boy's father said, he didn't say anything. "No Response" was the title of a photograph I'd taken of his face some years before this.

After we'd missed the light, we'd ride our bikes and go over how we had missed it.

Then we'd walk into the town for dinner at the diner-restaurant where our friends the chefs might be out in the alley smoking and also drinking beer, or wine out of a bottle they passed back and forth. Because they were in the restaurant drug world, they had used and abused many substances in their younger days. The sous-chef was still very young, not even thirty, though he pretended to be thirty when he was trying out seduction techniques on older women. He was so young that he didn't understand that thirty was as young as twenty-eight. Girls loved him because he looked like a boy in a comic strip and he had a forlorn expression when he wasn't laughing, smoking, or cooking. One night when

he was looking worried, he told me two bad dreams he'd had the
night before. He was like the lieutenant who told his dreams at
dinner in *The Discreet Charm of the Bourgeoisie,* but even funnier, telling dreams while cooking.

The way he looked when he cooked counted for a lot. He'd
place micro greens on top of the salad and then flick his hand
away as if he were doing a magic trick or conducting an orches-
tra. Next he'd stand back like a boy magician and look at the
tiny statue of leaves. "There!" he looked as if he was thinking.
He'd have a little smile on his face when he stood back. He didn't
think anyone was watching him, because all the diners were engaged in merriment and loud conversation. He could have any
girl he wanted in the whole town, just like Elvis Presley, and he
could cook. He would never order a bowl of gravy with dinner,
the way I'd read that Elvis liked to do.

One night he said to me, "Why don't you ever come for breakfast?"

"We can't eat those big breakfasts they serve here," I said. "I
don't understand going out for breakfast."

"Well, what do you have for breakfast?" he said.

"Steel-cut oats," I said. "Or kamut flakes with soy milk in
warm weather."

"I'll cook oatmeal for you," he said. No man had ever offered
to cook oatmeal for me. He probably went around offering to
cook anything for any girl he liked and it had turned into a reflex. Every day I had to face the fact that there was a new generation and that those for whom I'd babysat were taking over.

"But what are the camus flakes? Is it Albert Camus?" he asked.
He was a chef—he really wanted to know the answer.

"It's existential cereal," the other chef said as he took a puff of his cigarette. We all laughed, but then I remembered the photos of Camus smoking. This ended the fun.

Both chefs were wearing their white chef's jackets over shorts and big rolled-down socks and basketball sneakers. The younger one put stuff in his hair to make it stick out all over. The other one didn't bother with the sticking-out part but kept his hair slicked back in some other new style I hadn't yet been able to grasp. He had many girls in love with him, too.

I'd encountered one of these young women when I'd gone to the photo lab one night the year before to pick up some prints I'd taken of the cranberry bog. When the girl saw my name, she said that she recognized it from the book of photographs. "I didn't think people actually looked at the book," I said.

"Well, I used to go out with a chef who took it with him whenever we went on a trip off-island. He'd always read it on the ferry." When she said the chef's name she smiled, and I couldn't help seeing that her tongue was pierced. This pierced tongue ended the moment of happiness at the thought of the talented nihilist chef carrying the book around with him.

"It must be quite a feat to be his girlfriend," I said without thinking, and because I hadn't read Letitia Baldrige's etiquette advice in time to absorb and practice all the manners. The pierced girl blushed and said, "Yes, but I'm over it now." She was a member of the lucky generation that got over things.

I stopped by the restaurant on the way back to show the chefs the new photos of the cranberry bog. Everyone in Nantucket was interested in the colors of the bog. The sous-chef was there scrubbing the grill behind the counter, and I mentioned the meeting in the photo lab and what had just transpired.

"Oh, I know her," he said. "I like her."

"But what about the pierced tongue?" I said.

"I like that," he said.

"How could you like it?" I said.

"Guess," he said.

I tried guessing silently.

Then I said, "I don't see why they have to mutilate themselves."

"I believe in advancements in technology," he said. I looked at him and tried to take in the philosophy of those in his generation—the smoking, drinking, drug-using pierced young people.

"Did you know that women had to use vegetables before other, better things were invented?" he said.

I had heard Dr. Ruth Westheimer mention this on David Letterman's show, a decade or so ago, before Dave was used to the new crude society and civilization, and he appeared to be embarrassed.

"Were they at least organically grown vegetables?" I asked.

"They washed them first," he said. "Or peeled them too, maybe."

"But what about . . . ," I said, and then I couldn't say anything else. I looked at him and he looked at me. He was cleaning the stove and packing up the chopped ingredients and sauces. We both knew there was nothing else we could say.

The waiter passed by and said, "*What* are *you two talking* about?" Since he was almost forty, he still had some sense of decorum.

"We're talking about someone pierced," the sous-chef said.

"Which one?" the waiter asked. It could be any one of dozens, even on this tiny island.

"The one who went out with the boss," the sous-chef said. "The piercing was bothering someone. I'm training her to get over it."

"What a way to train someone," the waiter said as he continued in a merry way to the kitchen. Later on, I was told that the waitpersons liked to polish off the wine left over in all the bottles on the tables.

THE SMOKING chefs wanted us to come into the alley and talk to them on their nicotine-alcohol break. When I said, "But I can't breathe with the smoke in here," they took it as a joke.

"It's rough in there," the younger chef said about the un-air-conditioned restaurant and his work area behind the counter, where diners could watch the chefs cook and learn their fiery tricks. He said he needed to smoke to calm down.

"Isn't there some new drug medication that replaces nicotine?" I said.

"It's just some old thing like Prozac that the drug companies remarketed with a new name to get more money," he said, taking another puff and blowing the smoke up the alley.

"I heard that it works," I said. "And also the other stuff, the patches," I reminded him as he took more puffs and lit another cigarette right from the last butt.

"I need immediate relief," he said, inhaling. It was hard to watch.

"Why don't you do the yoga breathing, or take Xanax, or anything instead of nicotine?" I said. "Each puff does more damage." I was so tired of this conversation, I could barely say the words. I'd read that nicotine was more addictive than heroin.

"Do you have any Xanax?" the sous-chef asked.

"Of course I do," I said.

"What color?" he asked.

"Peach," I said.

"Peach is weak. I need blue," he said.

"Two peach equal one blue," I said. I saw that I was discussing colors of drugs and pills like an expert, in a back alley. But not exactly like that, because outside the alley were window boxes filled with white flowers, including white roses and trailing verbena.

"Do you have any Xanax with you?" he asked. "I'll trade you some baby vegetables we just got today."

"I don't carry them with me," I said. This was before the Event of September.

The chefs weren't surprised when I told them the story of the boy. They acted as if it were one of millions they knew. They feigned a bit of sympathy but continued with their competition to see who could do a better Sean Connery accent.

One sat on an empty vegetable crate, the other on top of an air conditioner. A six-foot-long carton was leaning against the brick wall. I'd seen it there for two weeks. A piece of cardboard with all colors of paint splattered on it was standing up next to it behind an old paint can.

"The last person who objected to our smoking is in this carton," the chef said.

Then they laughed. We laughed, too, even though I knew we were in a scene of depravity.

YOGA FOR THE HANDS

AFTER THIS INTERLUDE we walked to the bookstore. It was the only entertainment in the town. Even though there weren't many books, there were all the necessary books, and the manager liked to criticize the covers of the new ones. "Look at this, they're all dark brown! Why would they think they should be dark brown?" she'd say, pulling one out. "And last year they were all black. What's wrong with these art departments?"

I noticed a whole corner set aside for yoga books. They were serious books, not the new and fashionable ones which had been speeded out recently. A most unusual-looking and intentionally exotic woman dancer was on the cover of one of the books. She held her hands up in the air, thumb and index fingers touching.

Her hair was brown, pulled tight up and back, in an old-fashioned upsweep. Her penciled eyebrows were done in boomerang arches and she had a dramatic and all-knowing look on her face. In the pictures throughout the book she wore a series of crazy-looking dance outfits.

I had to pick up this book because of the six offers listed underneath the cover photograph. Number six, "Align your spirit and give yourself peace." The first one—"Eliminate fatigue and burnout"—seemed equally urgent.

Then, two through five: "Stop anxiety and depression," "Protect physical health," "Increase love and abundance," "Improve mental clarity and intuition." It was a need-all kind of invitation, like those horoscopes where everything applied to everyone.

Inside the book, the photographs of the dancer-author were more exotic. In some she'd let her long hair down, but all hanging on one side. Maybe the photographs were actually from the 1950s and she'd been doing the hand yoga the whole time, before it had caught on like wildfire in recent years. And since now there were more wildfires in California, she must have needed to add a quick new healing mudra for this kind of natural disaster. Listed in the table of contents was "Mudra for Healing After Natural Disasters."

On the first page of the book was a title, "Mudra for Healing a Broken Heart." That was my first priority. Then came "Overcoming Anxiety." That was my first priority, too. "Stronger Character"—if that were in place, the others wouldn't be necessary. "Healing the Mind"—that should be first.

The mudras started coming together in rapid succession. I'll buy the book and read it when I get home, I decided. The walk will calm everything down. But I couldn't make myself leave, and I stood in the bookstore under the hot bright spotlights in the track lighting, where I kept reading.

When I read the sentence "Rein in your wild thoughts and master your mind," I tried to disregard the appearance of the dancer in order to take her more seriously.

"Help with a Grave Situation," "Overcoming Addictions"—too late for that. "Pressure of the thumbs on the temples triggers a rhythmic reflex into the central brain and cures any addiction in thirty days." This had to be accompanied by "a short fast breath of fire." But I read on.

The next chapter was "Healing a Broken Heart," which would be needed in case the thumb pressure didn't work. I bought the book and ordered another one for the boy's father. I hoped he'd laugh when he looked at the photographs. But the boy himself would have had the time to go through the book discussing each costume and mudra.

The boy's father told me that he'd received the book. He laughed for a second. But then he asked, in a deep voice, without any expression, "Did you do the one for a broken heart?"

"Yes," I said, "but I haven't mastered the technique."

"Did you do the one for grief?" he asked.

"I tried them all," I said. "They were all versions of the same thing."

"Well, did they work?" he asked.

"They help you breathe and press the right spots for tranquillity."

"So, that's it—they don't help."

The truth was that the exercises were so complicated that when you tried to do them, while taking in the bizarre demonstration photos and costumes, you'd forget to think about why you were doing them. That was the cure.

THE WAY LIFE IS

W HEN WE WENT to Maine for a few days I heard a bit of philosophy that was the highlight of the summer.

I heard this when I went to the hardware store to buy a new fan to bring back to Nantucket. There were no fans left in any store on the island. We had seventeen fans in the rented house, but the square box fan lasts only one year before stopping—you plug it in one day and turn it on, nothing happens. You try different outlets, different speeds—nothing but silence and stillness and heat.

During the many heat waves, it was important to get to the hardware store the day the fan shipment arrived. Late at night you could go to the all-night supermarket, where you might be told, "The fan season is over for us. Next is the back-to-school season."

It's supposed to be cool in Maine, but it was hot. In the hardware store, there was only one fan going and it didn't keep the place cool enough for customers to stay there and buy more fans. Their one old fan was in operation on the counter. The grille of this fan was covered with thick gray dust. Longer pieces of the dust were hanging from the wires in a few spots.

I was waiting my turn to pay for the new fan I'd selected. I'd learned from past, hot experience that any fan on the shelf was the one to select. It was a short wait, because the store was well organized, with several cash registers and competent, well-trained cashiers.

I noticed the cashiers. They were an unhealthy-looking two-some. One was overweight in a flattened-out style going all over the place, no longer in the shape of a woman. The other had a puffy, suntanned face and wore her brown hair in braids tied up with red ribbons. The suntanned one said to her coworker, "How's your mother?"

"Better," was the answer, stated in a voice as flattened out as herself. "It's that manic-depressive thing," she explained.

"That runs on my side, too," the suntanned one said. "It's a chemical imbalance, you know," she added. Then she stopped a moment and said, "And also, the way life is."

AFTER THE SUMMER

Several months went by before the boy's mother left a message on my machine one day at seven P.M. It was only four P.M. in California.

That afternoon I had taken one low-dose orange Klonopin and one medium-dose peach Xanax. I was planning to lie down for a few minutes, until the high or low point of these two wore off.

If I fell asleep, I could wake up in time for us to go to the next town to see an English movie. But did I want to feel inferior to those upper-class English people and all their great stuff— mainly trees, hedges, giant bowls of flowers, flower-printed dishes, flower-printed upholstery—which they combined with their knowing how to be most cruel in a polite way?

We had an obsessive-compulsive friend. The friend was a scholar of French and English literature and she shared some symptoms with my other friends before she narrowed it all down to extreme anxiety.

"You need a drug to control this kind of thinking," she said to me no matter what I told her, including the fear of seeing English movies and the BBC news. "I've never heard of Anglophobia," she said.

She didn't mind taking what they call serotonin boosters, one after another, and also Klonopin, plus some other things she couldn't keep track of, to keep the boosters from being too powerful. Every week she took a different group of medications. One week her medicines didn't work and she spent a few days lying on her couch. While she was lying on the couch, I could walk a few miles.

When I couldn't find the camera I could plan for the next day's light. The camera might turn up in the canvas vitamin bag. I could talk to the woman who also walked the conservation land and liked to stop to discuss her knowledge of all kinds of plastic surgery. Tighten this, inject that, peel the other.

When the real terror happened, she'd discuss how she might still get to New York for appointments. "I'm afraid of the tunnel," she said.

"Take the bridge," I suggested. "Then you have a chance."

"No, on the bridge, if it goes down your neck breaks," she said.

"But in the tunnel you can't get out," I said.

"It's the flood of water rushing in," she said.

"No, it's the flames and smoke," I said.

"The water rushing in," she repeated, and demonstrated with her hands.

"The fire *and* the water," I said as I tried to walk away. "It's the end of the world."

"It was better when we discussed our faces," she said as she waved good-bye and walked off through the October-colored field.

. . .

BUT ONCE I heard the voice of the boy's mother, I couldn't fall asleep. She had such a lovely voice—young as a girl's, calm as a well-bred woman's—and to think that in a photo I'd seen of her as a teenager she looked like the teenager Justine who'd been a star on *American Bandstand* in 1961. She was prettier than Justine, and had a face as perfect as a doll's face. I heard her calm, poised, and lovely voice, without an accent of any kind. She kept that voice even though she'd gone to the same high school as Chubby Checker and Fabian. And now all this had happened to her life, and she still had kept the voice.

She had some questions. Had he ever discussed his drug use? No, only once, to say heroin was a good experience and that he'd do it over again if he could. And he'd recommend it to others. When he said that, I began to think he was still addicted. "I'd do it again"—that tipped me off. It was the day I told him about the unconventional, radical approach of the clinic in London where Marianne Faithfull stayed and was given heroin until she asked to be cured.

I told her everything he'd told me except things that might hurt her feelings. The fur coat was one of the things. It was a mink coat.

"What about this coat?" she'd asked me when I was visiting them in Boston. "My severest critic tells me to give it away." The boy had told me that she had traded something for it in an exchange with her furrier. A woman in my generation had a furrier and I was a supporter of PETA.

"My mother doesn't know what existentialism is," he'd said once. "I can't believe her not knowing these things."

"What color is her hair now?" I asked. I hadn't seen her since they'd moved to the other coast. I knew that he'd influenced her about hair color when he was in high school.

He thought for a second and said, "Red . . . blond . . . I can't remember."

SHE TOLD the history of the drugs starting with the summer. "First we couldn't find him for days," she said. "We flew to New York. It was around Labor Day weekend. We got to his apartment and found him there. The apartment was a mess."

I thought she meant laundry and unwashed glasses and dishes. "You mean disorganized?" I said.

"No. There was blood on the *ceiling* and blood on the *floor*! Splattered blood. He had blood on his shirt. There was no food at all in the refrigerator. He had track marks all up and down his arms. And he was acting as if everything was fine."

When she said "blood on the ceiling and blood on the floor" in her lovely, civilized voice, I tried to accept this in my mind as a picture, but I couldn't.

"You mean blood from injecting heroin?" I said. What did he think when he rolled up the sleeve of his perfectly pressed shirt? Right before that weekend, I had been talking to the boy, my friend, for all those hours. And now I knew what kind of room he was in at the time. Maybe during the all-night phone call, the yoga-ball call, blood was spurting all around the room in his amateur and desperate attempts to get a good vein. As I was pumping up the yoga ball, he might have been shooting up the heroin. I was an ignorant, naïve accomplice. I was a completely foolish person.

Then she told the long story, the ins and outs of all the rehabs, the story of the year I knew about from listening to the boy's father's telling of it, and also the parts the boy himself had told me. Now I knew it inside and out, from each angle.

The last two days of his life, she said, he cleaned up his room and washed his father's car. On the last night, they all three went to a Hollywood movie and out to dinner. Which movie? I forgot to ask. But his father had told me this movie detail before, with the name of it, and I thought that the movie might have been a contributing factor. When I said so, his father laughed. He laughed hard. But I was serious.

"After dinner, when we got home, Arnold said, 'I wonder why I haven't gotten my credit-card bill. I'm going to call them,' and he left the room. That was a signal. There was a second of silence. Then I heard the last words I'd ever hear from our son. He said, 'I'm going to get into my pajamas.' He went upstairs. I went to feed the dog and I folded some laundry. Then, when I didn't hear him, I went upstairs. I saw the bathroom door closed, and once we had a problem there before with him . . . injecting cocaine . . . so I called his name. I said it three times, each time louder and more frantically. When he didn't answer, I opened the door and he was on the floor.

"I ran out to the landing and tried to call Arnold, but I couldn't say his name. I tried to say it, but it wouldn't turn into his name. It was only a scream," she said. She gave a restrained imitation of a scream, three times, still calm, in her quiet, lovely voice.

"He thought the alarm had gone off. He ran upstairs. He saw him on the floor and did CPR, but it was too late. Then he called 911 and I did CPR. But it was no use."

I tried not to picture my friend dead in his pajamas on the bathroom floor. I tried not to picture his parents. They were my friends, too.

I felt these pictures going into my brain and changing the brain chemistry the way drugs were purported to do. In one of

Andrew Weil's books it says that thoughts alter brain chemistry as well as drugs altering thoughts. He believed in thinking good thoughts before resorting to psychopharmacology.

"He was afraid of the credit-card bill and that he'd be found out," the boy's mother said. "He never stole. He never borrowed. He ended his life because he couldn't stand that he was a heroin addict and what had become of him."

This sentence made me feel that I might start to cry. To keep us from both crying, we found a way to hang up. But then I thought she might be beyond crying by the way she'd told the story. It was more like a numb recitation, or "The Rime of the Ancient Mariner."

For years my husband had told me that all my friends were crazy. But now I saw a new stage, where my close friend had become a heroin addict and a suicide. It had to reflect on me, too.

The next day I called her back.

"Where was the dog?" I asked. But not right off the bat. I got up to it gradually.

"In the house," she said. "I don't remember."

What was the dog's response? I wanted to know. I asked her. But she couldn't remember anything about the dog.

Did the dog know what had happened? What did the dog know and when did he know it, I couldn't help wondering.

THE RED ROOM

I WENT OUTSIDE to walk and take some photographs of the light on the reeds growing up around the pond. After a while I thought about calling the boy's cousin. I'd thought about it for a few weeks. Then I did it. Soon we were into the whole thing—every part of it all at once and going back and forth to the different parts: the year, the three years, the childhood, the high school, the psychiatrists, the last year, the last weeks, the last weekend, the last days.

During one part we had this conversation:

"You don't want to know—how they discovered him using heroin," his cousin said.

"I do know. His mother told me. She said there was blood on the ceiling and on the floor."

"The room was covered with blood," he said.

I'd seen this look somewhere. It popped into my mind. A photograph in *Vogue* magazine in a dentist's office, maybe a room color favored by a person who was one of their favorite people to feature; or a room wallpapered by a male designer—red velvet wallpaper, red carpet, and red velvet ceiling. The pictures of red rooms I'd seen in waiting-room magazines were shocking in a different way and were stored in a nearby part of the brain—the color section.

Then the boy's cousin mentioned a book he was reading. His generation had been taught to respect bad writers by the academics of my generation, who had been influenced by the academics of the generation before. To change the subject, I asked whether he had read anything by the Swiss writer Robert Walser.

"Oh yes, I know about him." He said that he'd read about the writer in an essay by the philosopher Walter Benjamin.

"What's the essay?" I asked.

"I can't remember," he said. "It's in a book, either *Illuminations* or *Reflections*."

I wrote it down on a scrap of paper. Then he said he had to hang up.

HOLY NIGHT

I T WAS A holy night. The stars were shining brightly, or brightly shining. Icy-cold winter air came back, "courtesy of the northwest cold front," the weather forecaster said. I felt it was a special courtesy directed to me, personally, since most people didn't share the joy of it. I liked to look at the weather map, one of the only beautiful sights on television. I was glad to see the white, snowy arrow of cold, the white stars under the white cloud, the snowflakes, the minus signs, the single digits, the curved wind signal for the front rushing in from Canada, where the better air was stored, and the deep blue and green of the oceans and the states. The states were all depicted without showing what was in them: cars, highways, gas stations, factories, tall buildings, industrial parks, malls, and overweight humans in tight pants and T-shirts. It was a peaceful and calming picture inspiring the meditative frame of mind, even though I still hadn't learned how to meditate.

A Chinese acupuncturist had punctured a number of needles into my shoulder—thicker needles than those I was used to with an international specialist. Then he turned a hot red spotlight in the direction of the needles and ran from the room saying, "Close eyes. Meditate."

I said I didn't know how.

"Not too much thinking," he said as he scurried out the door.

The icy weeks of winter weren't going to last, and I knew I had to pack every moment of the coldness into each day and night. I'd already been to the all-night supermarket and T.J. Maxx once, at nine P.M., and the experience was so delightful that I planned to go back for another trip.

I was the only customer at the discount clothing store. When I drove into the empty parking lot, I saw that the store was empty, too, and I was afraid they'd closed early due to extreme winds and icy blasts. Six or seven shopping carts had been blown over and were lying in a random pattern of beauty in my path. They looked so much better lying on the ground than standing up. Maybe the pattern of the carts signified a warning of dangerous weather reports I hadn't heard. Maybe it signified nothing, as Macbeth said.

I forged on ahead toward the vast, empty space of the store. The store looked better than it had in a few months. It seemed to have been emptied of most of the merchandise, and the remaining garments had been consolidated in the center of the white vinyl-tiled floor. A rack with a sign reading LONG-SLEEVED SHIRTS had become a rack with skirts, slacks, sweaters, and shirts. Only one employee could be seen—a young man with shoulder-length hair and bangs. People were afraid of him until they discovered how polite and helpful he was.

The same thing had happened with the all-tattooed cashier at
the supermarket. He even said hello. Maybe that was the hidden
meaning of the supermarket's Christmas commercial, which
showed a holiday table of food, fruit, lit candles, and a message
that read, "Wishing a happy holiday from our family to yours."

I wondered what was meant by the supermarket's "family." Of
whom did it consist? The store looked nothing like the commercial's depiction of a holiday home. The tattooed cashier may have
been one part. Then, at Christmas, there was a new member of
the family. An African-American woman was wearing a red Santa
Claus hat and standing at the cash register. She had an accent and
expression in her voice I hadn't heard since my childhood; now
I heard it when watching documentaries about the South. She
was from the Mississippi or Alabama or Tennessee of the past.
She sounded like a member of a jazz or blues group from the
fifties—beaten down, trying to get up, discriminated against,
all-knowing and resigned at the same time. She was addressing
the customers with the names "honey" and "sweetie pie."

"I'm so tired," she said. "I'm just praying to God I make it
through."

When my turn came, I felt sorry for her and had to ask, "Do
they make you wear the red hat?"

"No, that's from my other job, at the drugstore," she said.

All I could say was "Oh." Because this was her life, working
around the parking-lot chain stores, one after another.

"Man, those crackers are good," she said, picking up a package of Parmesan crisps. "Have you had them?" she asked me.

"They're too spicy for me," I said. I didn't want to get into the
discussion. I'd heard of people regretting having eaten an entire
package of the rich, spicy crisps.

"Well, you try them, you hear?" she said. "You won't believe how good they are."

By then I had packed up my own items, including organic kale and Desert Essence Tea Tree Shampoo, into a paper bag, and she said, "Thank you for packing." Even though I always packed, instead of "You're welcome," I said, "You were tired," but it didn't sound quite right.

"I am tired," she said. "I'm so tired I could drop down right here. So thanks again, sweetheart."

"You're welcome," I said.

THE HOLY nights are good for getting things done around the town. Only one or two people are out.

On my next visit, the supermarket's parking lot was almost empty. As I got out of the car, I felt that frigid air they kept warning about on the Weather Channel. The new bad thing they have on the channel is a diagram showing and telling viewers what to wear for the weather. On hot days in November, before it cooled off, they were still showing and announcing short sleeves, shorts, sunglasses, caps with visors. This was right before Thanksgiving. In the cold weather they say, "Sweater, heavy coat, gloves, scarf, hat," and show small computerized pictures of the garments, too. This is one of the bad parts of the Weather Channel.

As I walked toward the entrance, past the empty parking spaces, I heard two birds suddenly start chirping into the cold night. Maybe they were shocked out of sleep, or just desperate from their inability to find some warm evergreen branches for their night.

.   .   .

WHEN I returned on an icy night just before Martin Luther King Jr. Day, there was the same cashier, this time in a white knit cap with a white faux-fur trim. I assumed it was her own hat, but then realized that it might be the drugstore's winter-theme cap.

"Are you feeling any better?" I asked her.

"Sure I am. Last time I had just got out of the hospital. I had an aneurysm and a heart attack. That's why I was tired."

"Which hospital?" I asked.

She named the small local hospital.

"Go to the university hospital," I said.

"I know it, honey," she said. "They don't know nothing at this place. I said, 'I'm getting out of here!' My friends and relatives prayed for me, that's why I'm alive. That place! They are confused!"

I wanted to ask her about her past—how long she'd been here, where she was from, what kind of jobs she'd had before, all that. What I really wanted to understand was how she was still speaking in that accent and style and why she was stuck in these jobs. There it was, Martin Luther King weekend, and no improvement for the plight of this woman and others like her. Because of the sadness of this, I didn't ask her anything more.

Then she picked up the Parmesan crisps and said, "These crackers are so good!"

"Last time I was here you told me that, remember?" I said.

"And wasn't I right? They better be good for seven dollars."

They must be good if so many people had experiences with them, I was thinking, and now this poor downtrodden cashier, aneurysm and all, was still remarking on their excellence.

"Pray for me, sweetheart," she called in my direction as I left. I said I would. And I'd add something to the prayer about help-

ing her not eat too many Parmesan crisps. Among the ingredients, butter was listed, along with Parmesan cheese.

I WAS able to speed right through T.J. Maxx nearby and see
that there was nothing to buy. "Get in, and get out" was the
motto everyone had for the place. During the five years of trips
to the store, I'd purchased only three shirts and eleven pairs of
socks.

I'd been scared away for a week after having seen some dec-
orated bell-bottom blue jeans. On these blue jeans there was
everything possible, including long pieces of wool sewn on and
hanging from the waist, trouser bottoms, and pockets. Just six
pieces of wool—black, orange, brown, red, green, and blue.
Then came sequins, glitter, appliqués, embroidery, metal spikes
and studs—everything sewn on, stapled in, or hanging from
these pants. I noticed the sign on the display rack: EUROPEAN DE-
SIGNER JEANS. I tried to imagine who the European designer could
be: Yves St. Laurent, Karl Lagerfeld, Sonia Rykiel, Valentino,
Ungaro, Versace. But perhaps Europe included Poland, Slovenia,
and Yugoslavia and the designer was from one of these countries, or from what's called an outlaw state.

I was relieved to see that the manager was absent. When she
was there, her voice, in range between a squeak and a shriek,
could be heard throughout the store. I checked for the usual
placement of the "designer jeans" on my way out. The song
on the radio was unidentifiable, but something like a torture
to force prisoner spies to tell government secrets, and this was
speeding up my journey to the exit door. I'd left the store on another occasion when I heard the words from a song. "Lay down
beside me" were the words.

I wondered what had been done with the "designer jeans"—had they been shipped off to Africa? Thrown in a Dumpster? Left on the doorstep of a thrift shop? Dumped in a vacant lot and burned? Burned in effigy with our flag in one of the many countries where America was hated?

Outside, alone in the cold and empty parking lot, I heard the roar of the outdoor cleaning truck. The truck seemed to have grown to twice the size it had been—the many thick wheels in front and back had increased in size and number, and now the center had been displaced by a twisted black machine: an external motor-engine resembling a monster from a science fiction movie.

EVERY TIME I went out the door of our house I was happy. The sky was lit up with an almost full moon, but it was so clear that the large extra-bright stars were visible. I don't know the names of stars or stellar constellations. The same goes for the new movie stars. In astronomy, there was too much to think about. A friend of ours compulsively said the names of the stars whenever we went out walking at night, but people who named movie stars were worse to be around.

Naming the stars interferes with absorbing the night. These are the nights that teachers in schools try to re-create for Christmas pageants—deep, dark blue, with starlight and moonlight, without cars or humans. These are the holy nights. Holy night came into my mind, not the song but the scenery. The Christmas carol always reminded me of a grade-school Christmas concert from my childhood. My role was to hit the chime in one part of the musical score and at every rehearsal I missed the right moment.

Finally, I was demoted out of the important, chime-playing position. The music teacher had once held such high hopes for my role in the recital. Only Paul Shaffer's annual imitation of Cher singing "O Holy Night" on the David Letterman show could counteract the memory.

RETURN TO THE
WAXER-ELECTROLOGIST

O<small>N THIS HOLY NIGHT</small> of moonlight, frigid air, emptiness, starlight, and peace, I was still on the way to the waxer-
electrologist. She had told me she'd spent years destroying the
hair follicles of one of her clients. She'd shared the job with another electrologist in California, where the client lived part of
the year. "Between the two of us, it took nine years," she said.
She was serious, but I was laughing.

"People have these problems," she said. "You don't know because yours is minor in comparison."

She might start talking about more extreme cases and go
on to explaining the meaning of "hermaphrodite." She liked
to explain things even if the meanings of the things were well
known. She often told stories with grotesque details I didn't care
to know. The cold weather gave her ideas of tales to tell—for
example, swans' feet froze the swans into the ponds before they
could fly off to safety.

After I threw myself down onto the table, we started talking about other things—in addition to the life of the follicle. During our last appointment, we'd discussed the difficulty in finding medical specialists in the small town where we lived. We got to the specialty of psychotherapy.

"The only good ones are retired or dead," I'd said.

"There aren't many good ones on the planet," she said.

This gave me a sudden new respect for her, even as she stuck the electrology needle into my skin, between the eyebrows, at a voltage I'd asked her to lower many times. She was always sneaking it up for a longer-lasting attack on the follicle.

On this visit I told her I had just seen one of the five worst psychiatrists I'd ever seen in my life, beginning at age eighteen.

"Why?" she asked. She sounded fascinated, thoroughly engaged, on the edge of her electrology seat.

I described the office of one of the five worst psychiatrists— a large overdecorated parlor in a big color-coordinated house. Then came the psychiatrist herself, who was dressed in the style of a matron from a suburb. The shoes alone were a bad sign. They were a bad version of Gucci loafers from the 1960s, with a higher heel and shiny gold buckles. Her clothing—if only the boy had been around to hear about this, I forgot to think at the time but realized a few days later. The whole getup was a watered-down copy of something else—so weak a copy you couldn't tell what had been copied. The suit, if it could be called a suit, was a version of a Chanel suit but without anything to mark it as such. All that remained of the style was a short jacket and a plain skirt. The doctor's method of treatment derived from the Daytime TV School of Therapists.

I told the electrologist, "Every few minutes she'd say, 'How can I be of help to you?'"

"Oh, that is ridiculous," the electrologist said. "That's terrible! 'How can I help you?' That's for her to figure out."

"When someone goes to a cardiologist with chest pains do they ask, 'How can I help you?' This is what I mean, it's not even a profession. There are no standards."

She was up to the stage of pulling the wax strips off my ankles and I could see her taking a break to stand still and shake her head back and forth.

The electrologist asked whether the psychiatrist had made any other contribution to the appointment other than "Tell me, how can I be of help?" I remembered the other question she'd begun with. That was the moment I should have left. But it was seven degrees outside and I had arranged to be picked up from the long, ice-covered driveway in an hour. "She started by saying, 'I'm going to ask you a question that may surprise you.' I was prepared for a real surprise, but she said, 'Tell me three things you like about yourself.' "

"Oh my God," the waxer said as she tore another strip of waxing cloth off my leg. "How stupid! What did you say to that?"

"I said, 'I can't think of any.' "

I was watching her try to get off every last bit of wax. She was patting the skin and dabbing the cloth strips over every tiny spot. She was working so hard I wanted to tell her: Look, it doesn't matter if you leave some wax on. I don't care. I'm not going anyplace. I'll peel it off later, in the shower.

"These psychotherapists have no idea about the artistic temperament," she said. "They have the most middle-class values."

"Oh, you understand that."

"I do," she said. "Of course, ultimately, we're all alone, every one of us. But we need some guidance."

. . .

NOT ONLY did the waxer know more than most psychotherapists but she could also wax and destroy follicles at the same
time. I was lying down—the position Freud found conducive for
patients to do their talking—except when turned over to wax
the back of the legs, which would be less conducive. The Chinese acupuncturist had told me to lie down on my back after
he'd stuck the needles all over, into my shoulders. "My patients
do this," he'd said.

"But what about the needles?" I asked.

"Don't worry," he'd said. "Fine with the needles."

Maybe he was from the school of lying on a bed of nails, the
way magicians used to do on *The Ed Sullivan Show*. But that
technique took years of training. I wasn't going to lie down on
the acupuncture needles, that was definite.

"I've written a paper on 'Creative Genius,' " I heard the electrologist say. "When I was in school," she said. "Because of my
lifelong interest in the arts."

There were examples of her artwork all around, needlepoint
pictures of animals and quilts with scenes in nature. "I love grass
and trees, woods and forests, hills and rivers," wrote Michael
Powell, the director of *The Red Shoes*, my other favorite movie,
in his autobiography. And the waxer loved these things in nature
too, even though she wasn't an aristocratic English film director. She painted and drew; she needlepointed and quilted leaves,
grass, rocks, raindrops, flowers, orchids, sand, ice, water—
everything loved by Michael Powell, Keats, Wordsworth, Percy
Bysshe Shelley, William Robinson, Gertrude Jekyll, and millions of others, including Wallace Nutting and Frederick Law
Olmsted, in our own country.

I decided not to bring up *The Red Shoes*, or any movie. She had recommended some foreign-film videos to me when I said we didn't go to Hollywood movies and just watched old ones over and over.

I had reported to her that one of her recommended foreign films was too sad. "You didn't tell me it had an unhappy ending."

"You need it to have a happy ending?" she said as she got her needle ready. "Why?"

"There's enough misery everywhere," I said. "You know that I watch David Letterman and reruns of *SCTV*."

"What about depth?" she said.

"They're deep," I said.

Then the electrologist said, "What about profundity?"

What about it? Was it a word? "There's enough of that everywhere, too," I said. It was better to watch Gene Kelly dance in the rain than a movie about poor Arabs collecting flower petals and riding donkeys over bridges in floods.

"What about the visual, the cinematography?" she said.

I thought about the fields of flowers. But I wasn't over the ending and I told her so.

I got up from the table. As I was rubbing on some aloe vera gel, I noticed one of the six old cats sitting all crouched up on a chair. He was looking out at nowhere.

"What must he be thinking is going on in here?" I asked.

"Oh, he's old. He's not thinking," the electrologist said. "The other cats intimidate him. That's why he's in here."

I tried touching the cat's head, but he didn't look any happier. "At least you don't have to have electrolysis and waxing," I said to him.

"Animals get insecure the way people do," the electrologist said. "That's his problem. They have feelings too."

FACES OF PETS

As I drove home, I was thinking about an acquaintance who had cats and dogs she'd gotten from shelters near her house in Maine. She and her children had some other animals they'd found here and there. When I was last at their house, her mutt-like, rough, spiky-furred dog was around everywhere and barking for no reason.

"Look at that face," she'd said. "See, the face of unconditional love. Isn't it great?"

"I want conditional love," I said. "I want to be loved only for good things I do."

"Why?" she said. "Look at that face." She touched the mutt-face.

I looked at the dog's face. I didn't get the whole picture of the love affair.

On the white armchair was a freaky-looking gray cat with

white whiskers. The pet owner said the cat's name. I heard it to be Witch.

"Witch?" I said, looking at the evil witchy-looking little cat.

"Mitch, not Witch," the owner said while laughing. "Mitch is very old and weak," she explained. If he was so old, why was he so small? Maybe he was an actual cat midget.

I knew what old and weak meant, but I put it out of my mind and went on to look at the next animal—a huge, spreading, gray, long-furred cat, who'd taken over the territory on the white bed-spread.

"Is he blind?" I said, looking at his half-closed eyes that showed cataracts, glaucoma, or eyeliner around the lids.

"No, he had glaucoma when we found him under a bridge. We cured him," she said in a confident way. The cat blinked those weird eyes. "We took him to a vet and he got every medi-cine there was." As I looked at the cat and listened to his medical treatments, I thought about the sick people in other countries and about why people in those countries hated Americans.

IN IRAN, I'd read, dog owning was a sin or a crime, especially small-dog owning. Dogs were considered to be dirty—one point of agreement with the Iranian fundamentalists. In Reykjavík, Iceland, dogs were banned because of all kinds of problems they caused for everyone other than their owners. But in a film I'd seen on PBS, one of Shackleton's men loved a dog so much he said the dog was a better companion than some humans. I saw the man trying to kiss the dog. That was fun—to watch an En-glishman on Shackleton's expedition showing true love for his dog's frozen, furred face. The English would rather kiss a dog than a person in public.

The cat was lying on the bed like a king, as if he owned it. Maybe this was how people came to give their pets those creepy names like Queenie and Princess. The cat owned the bed, the room, the view of the garden, and the whole house, I could tell.

"We love him so much we won't let him go outside," the cat owner said. She seemed pleased by the situation.

I reviewed relationships I'd known between people and cats—cats wanted food. Dogs, too. You gave them food and touching, they loved you for it. They'd love anyone who gave them food. Pet owners don't want to know that. If they did, they'd have a truthful emptiness the way I had.

Then, as I was seeing this cat and dog picture, I thought about relationships between people. I thought about cooking. I had grown to hate cooking, even though I was learning new vegetarian-sauce tips from the two chefs in Nantucket. The worst part is where pieces of vegetables fall onto the floor and you have to pick them up in the midst of cooking, and also the bent-over searching for things in the low refrigerator drawer. This gave a scullery-maid feeling. The real chefs have people picking up for them after the cooking is done and also preparing and chopping before it's started.

My husband had never peeled a carrot in his life. Whatever work I was doing when he put his gigantic sandwich together with ounces of mayonnaise—at least it was eggless mayonnaise—I had to stop everything to wash and peel a carrot and cut it up. He never got the idea to eat an apple when he was hungry. "If you want me to eat fruit, you have to cut it up," he'd said about some cantaloupe in the refrigerator when he was forty-four. This applied to apples and other small, easy fruit as well.

I thought of all those carrots. If I didn't have the carrot ready, he'd eat more bread, or a cookie made with hydrogenated fats, a cookie that he'd bought by himself. Once when I put a carrot on his desk, when he was in his last good mood in several years, he said, "The carrot of love." He didn't care that it was the carrot of lutein-lycopene.

I looked at the two cats and the one ruffian mutt, who was giving a bark here and there while lurching about the room. How exactly was animal loving different from love between human beings, I was thinking. The cat blinked those scary black-lined, half-stuck eyelids.

I thought of the negotiations with my husband over the fruit and vegetables and the doing this and that for each other. I thought of his face. I looked at it—he was standing next to me in the pet-filled room—the face of a kindly stranger. And I was like Blanche DuBois, dependent on the kindness of strangers and unable to stand the sight of a bare lightbulb. It had taken five years to get him to agree to ceiling lamp shades in the laundry room.

I'd been dependent on the kindness of the other stranger, the boy—strange, stranger than anyone, and a stranger to everyone.

I looked at the faces of the pets—are they called faces?—and I wondered what the nature of the relationships could be.

Was this what the boy meant by low self-esteem and pity? I needed his help to remember.

ACKNOWLEDGMENTS

The author wishes to thank the John Simon Guggenheim Foundation for supporting her work.

ABOUT THE AUTHOR

JULIE HECHT is the author of *Happy Trails to You*; *Do the Windows Open?*, a collection of stories, all of which appeared in *The New Yorker*; and *Was This Man a Genius?*, a book of talks with Andy Kaufman. She has won an O. Henry Prize and a Guggenheim Fellowship. She lives on the east end of Long Island in the winter and in Massachusetts in the summer and fall.

Printed in the United States
By Bookmasters